PEPPED UP & WILDER

ALI DEAN

Chapter One

PEPPER

I hardly recognize the woman in the full-length mirror staring back at me. She's wearing a long black dress with a slit mid-thigh. The front plunges down to expose the space between her breasts and a flash of abs, but despite the show of skin, the expensive material and elegant straps scream sophistication. I turn to the side, taking in the way the fabric clings to the butt in the mirror, the exposed back with a wicked sports bra tan line. I sigh in relief at the familiarity of those lines on my back. Is it weird that the imperfection to this getup is comforting to me?

In the mirror, I watch as a man in a tuxedo walks into the bedroom of the hotel suite. As he moves toward me, I imagine we're in one of those cheesy commercials for diamonds or expensive jewelry. I'm embarrassed for us. We're not glamorous people. It's like we're playing dress-up.

"What are you giggling about, Mrs. Wilder?" I love when Jace calls me that. There was no Mrs. Wilder growing up, so it's not weird. It's my own. But it's Jace's too.

"Who *are* we right now?" I ask. Jace's hands slide around my hips and I lean back into his chest as we gaze at our reflections.

"I don't know about you, but I feel like James Bond in this thing."

My smile widens. "I know. Right? It feels like a costume. I don't even really look like me."

"You're still you," he says, his lips dropping to my neck. "Just another gorgeous version. Running clothes, pajamas, designer dress, it's all a tease to me. A reminder that I'm the luckiest guy in the world."

When Jace says things like this, I remember how far we've come. The boy who was too scared to admit his feelings to himself, much less to me, has grown into a man who gushes adorations with such sincerity, I'll never doubt the depth of his love for me.

I turn away from the mirror and look up into green eyes I know better than my own. They darken as his hands slide over the back of my dress, caressing my bottom.

"I've missed you," I admit.

Jace pulls me closer so I'm flush against him.

"I know." Jace lets out a small sigh. "Football season is over. But between all the events and endorsement stuff I've got lined up and your race schedule..." He drifts off, and my head drops to his shoulder. There's no end in sight.

"We're both doing what we love. I just wish it didn't keep us apart so much." I say the words to his tux jacket. It's hard to admit to myself that the distance and our chosen career paths are hard. Really hard. I thought we had everything we could ever want, and I feel like a whiner complaining about it. The truth is, I wonder how long we can both chase our dreams before we break. Our love for each other runs deep, but we have huge ambitions in our sports. I don't know what the answer is, if there even is one. For now, I simply cherish the time we have together before one of our commitments pulls us apart again.

"I'm doing all I can to get traded to the Stallions, Pep." Jace just completed his third season playing for the Browns in Cleveland. He was the second-string quarterback but had the opportunity to play at several games. Though Jace made an impression when he got game time, the first-string quarterback for the Browns isn't planning to retire anytime soon. Jace is in a good position to trade to another team looking for a new quarterback. It's a long shot he'll get the team he wants in Colorado though, with so much of the politics involved out of his control.

Still, we just moved back to Brockton for the off-season. He'll be around a lot more without games nearly every week. It will be a solid four or five months of mostly living together without too much travel.

I feel a buzz at my hip, and Jace keeps one hand on me while checking the phone in his pocket with the other. "Frankie's waiting for us downstairs."

Jace holds me a moment longer. I want him to kiss me, but I just applied lipstick. Heat fizzles between us. "We should go," I finally say.

"Stay close tonight, okay?" he asks before releasing me.

"You know I will."

"Sometimes you drift off when I get stuck in a conversation or interview. I know they drag on, but stay by my side, okay?"

"I don't drift off," I correct him. "The crowds swarm and I get pushed back. You'll have to hold me tighter to keep me from getting swept away," I tease. Maybe I do let myself drift off a little. Jace has to turn into an actor at these publicity events, and he doesn't feel like mine in those moments. He belongs to the whole world, the fans whose numbers have skyrocketed astronomically since he got field time last season. The NFL is buzzing with talk of Jace Wilder and where he'll land next season.

Jace lets me go so I can grab my clutch and the heavy shawl I'm supposed to wear instead of a jacket. He has a team of people and someone named Janet, whom I've never met, sends me clothes for these black-tie fundraisers. I don't have to pay for the clothes and I never know what to do with them afterward since I won't wear them again. The designers who provide these dresses have a marketing strategy, knowing I'll get photographed by Jace's side and that the images and my outfit will show up all over the internet. It's February but apparently a jacket would ruin the look this designer is going for, so a shawl it is.

As he takes my hand and leads me out to the elevators, I realize that he's not the only one who turns into an actor when we step into the public eye. I'm playing a part, too.

Alone in the elevator with Jace, we're good. We're us. We smirk at each other as the energy crackles between us, daring one another not to make a move. I had my hair professionally styled hours earlier, and

Jace's tux is perfectly pressed, so we manage to be good until the doors open.

Jace's arm slips around my waist as we walk out to the hotel lobby. Frankie's hard to miss at three hundred pounds of solid muscle. His fiancée Lizzie is beside him, and they grin as we approach.

The guys rib each other about cleaning up nice before complimenting one another's girl. Frankie is a defensive lineman for the Stallions. Despite playing for a rival team, he's remained one of Jace's closest friends. The event tonight is a kick-off fundraiser for a charity he just founded, and it's a bit of a risky move for Jace to attend. The hotel a few blocks down the street, where we are headed now, will be filled with Stallions players, coaches, and their supporters. While it's unusual for a player from a rival team to attend, it's common knowledge that Frankie and Jace were roommates and teammates in college. And after tonight, the whispers that Jace has his heart set on the Stallions for a trade will be common knowledge as well.

We'd thought that arriving by foot would attract less attention than pulling up in front of the building in a car and stepping right into the flashing cameras. We were wrong. Despite the dozens of other large athletes arriving, it's hard not to notice two of them strolling down the sidewalk in tuxes. Even in the inky night, it's like there's a spotlight shining down on us.

One camera flash is followed by another, and another, until I'm so blinded I can barely walk forward. Jace's arm around my waist tightens and I do my best to plaster a smile on my face that doesn't look like a grimace. Someone seems to be clearing the way because we manage to get inside the doors, and then we're in another fancy hotel lobby, this one significantly more crowded than the one where we're staying. We're ushered over to an actual red carpet with backdrops displaying the logo for Frankie's foundation, which will provide funds for research on Alzheimer's treatment.

We endure more photographs, this time staged. Frankie is the main attraction of the night, with the focus on his foundation, which is named after his paternal grandmother. Still, it's no surprise Jace's presence creates a stir. He's prepared for the questions and replies just as he's been coached, without providing too much information.

As promised, I remain close to Jace's side, and he keeps his arm wrapped around me throughout the interviews. I don't question why it's so important I stay close. He's good at this, playing the celebrity. From Brockton Public to UC, he's been slowly training for this kind of recognition and spotlight. It's a new level of fame but not entirely foreign. Still, I know that he likes showing the world that we're a united front. That his celebrity status doesn't come in a vacuum. So many of the players, especially the younger ones like Jace, are fawned over for their bachelor status. Jace makes it clear he's a married man, and proud of it, and I love him for it.

I wonder too, as I glance around the lobby, noting the several tall supermodels interspersed amongst other players' wives trying to keep up, if Jace wants me by his side to protect me. Does he worry when I drift off that I can't take care of myself? Not only has the level of spotlight increased exponentially, but it seems the other aspects that follow Jace's world have as well. Petty or obsessive women, jealous men who feel threatened by Jace, they still exist here, even if in theory people should be older and more mature than our high school and college days. Only now, there's more on the line. More money, more power. Rings on our fingers haven't deterred all the women, only brought out the more determined ones, set on snagging the next NFL star.

I almost feel sorry for them. We've been through so much together, I can handle anything. They don't know who they're dealing with.

Chapter Two

PEPPER

It shouldn't be a surprise that Troy Bremer is the first person we see when we finally leave the lobby and enter the ballroom. With hundreds of people in attendance, he's easily the most famous one here tonight. He might even be the most famous person in the entire state. Troy and his wife, Stephanie, haven't made it very far into the room and are surrounded by people seeking their attention.

Troy is the Stallions' current quarterback. Rumor has it that next season will be his last. Jace could work with the team under Troy for a season before, hopefully, moving into the starting QB position.

His wife spots us first, and greets us with a megawatt smile.

"Jace and Pepper! So wonderful you joined us this evening." Her tone is a bit effusive, her voice overly loud as she spreads her arms and draws attention. The group surrounding the Bremers turns to look at us.

I roll my shoulders, reminding myself to continue playing the part. Jace remains in publicity mode as he greets her. "Ms. Bremer, it's nice to see you again. This is my wife, Pepper."

I was at the US track and field championships last summer when Jace attended a function that the Bremers were at as well. They've only met on the one occasion.

"Oh, please. Call me Stephanie." She greets us with hugs, as if we've known each other for years. Except I don't get warm vibes. Is this part of the show? Jace seems to be playing along as he gives Troy's hand a friendly shake.

Stephanie maintains an overly loud voice when she asks, "Isn't it so lovely Pepper could make it tonight? I'm sure with your racing schedule you don't get to attend many events with Jace. Or watch his games," she adds. It's an odd statement, and I quickly erase the frown forming between my brows. Was that a dig or is she trying to make conversation? I'm always on high alert, suspicious, when we're in celebrity mode.

Troy ignores his wife's comment and compliments Jace on the four games he played in last season. The conversation turns to football, and a few others join. While I don't exactly follow the players' relationship status, it's common knowledge that the Bremers are high school sweethearts. They got married at eighteen and just celebrated a twenty-year anniversary. The brief news snippet about it caught my attention, if only because it was comforting to hear about other high school sweethearts like me and Jace.

Watching the way Troy ignored his wife, and how he now seems to be ignoring me, my feelings on the matter shift. Perhaps they aren't the kind of couple I should be looking up to as an example. As I lean into Jace and listen to comments about his potential by the strangers circling around us, Stephanie brushes against my arm.

She flashes another broad smile my way and tilts her head to the side. I think it's a gesture indicating I should step her way so we can chat about something other than football. Keeping my fingers intertwined with Jace's, I shift my body away from the group so that I'm facing Stephanie, who's been pushed outside the circle.

"So, tell me, Pepper." Her voice has dropped to a low purr, and if she hadn't already put me on edge, I'm now on full alert. "Are you planning to continue running professionally?"

Her head bends toward mine, like she's conspiring with me about something.

"Yes, of course," I answer, not suppressing my perplexed tone. "My career has only just begun."

"I see." She nods, putting a finger to her chin in contemplation. "Now, if Jace becomes first-string quarterback, you won't keep traveling around the world for your own races, will you?"

My eyes narrow at her audacity. Sure, her tone sounds friendly, but patronizing too. "Um." I pause, uncertain how to continue. I decide to pretend like she's interested in my career. "I'm going to be moving away from cross country, which entails more international racing, and moving into road races. Marathons and half marathons. Most of my races will be in the States and because they are longer distances, I won't be competing quite as often." My training cycles will demand more from me though, and I may even need to travel for some of the harder blocks, depending on where Jace lands.

Stephanie takes my arm and pulls me from Jace so we're alone, hiding behind our husbands. Clearly, she has something she wants to say to me. We're here to create good vibes between Jace and the Stallions, so I'll have to endure it.

"Pepper, sweetie, I admire your running talent. I really do." Yes, all patronizing now. "But let me give you some advice. The NFL isn't like high school. It's nothing like college. I dated the quarterback in high school, was with Troy through the college years too. I know what it's like to have other women trying to take what's yours. It's unavoidable."

I soften a tiny bit in sympathy. Obviously, we've shared some experiences.

She continues, "You've probably had a little taste of what it's like in the pros. The women are more obsessed, there's more money on the line, and some of them have zero morals."

I nod. "Oh, I know." She's not telling me anything new here, but I humor her, listening with wide eyes like she's being very helpful.

"It will only get worse once he's first string. Now, what you might not realize yet is that most of these players, whether they are married or not, take full advantage of the women who want them." She pauses, watching for a reaction I refuse to give her. "Jace might have denied the temptation up to this point. You're newlyweds after all, and the women aren't flocking to him as heavily as they will once he's first string, but," she pauses again, this time, I'm guessing, for dramatic effect, "he won't be able to resist forever. He's a man, after all."

I try not to react at her insult but my face scrunches up in distaste. So Troy cheats on his wife and she's bitter about it? What is she trying to prove? I'm much wiser than I once was and right now, I need to know her angle. She's pretending to give advice, but I know there's an ulterior motive.

She pats my arm. "If you want to keep your marriage together, sweetheart, you need to let your running ambitions go. After all, it's not as if you're an Olympian. Your husband must make astronomically more than you ever will. You need to start thinking about shifting your focus. If you want your marriage to last, if you want him to keep *seeing* you, you need to be at his side at all times. Otherwise, you'll start to drift away and be replaced by the younger women when you're gone."

Younger women? I'm only twenty-three, almost twenty-four, but still. Okay, she clearly has a huge chip on her shoulder. I don't think this woman has an agenda so much, or anything against me, she seems to simply have a truckload of emotional baggage, grief and jealousy and is unloading it on me. Wanting me to carry some of the burden. If her husband is on his way out of the pros, and their marriage is in shambles, perhaps she has some regrets. Had she tried going after her dreams and her husband strayed?

I decide to ask her. "Did you have something you wanted that you went after before Troy went pro?"

Her eyes flutter. "Of course not. I knew in high school what my role would be. I was a cheerleader, and while I'm not holding pompoms or wearing a ruffled skirt these days, that's still my role. It has to be."

My stomach drops. Not for me, but for her. She never let herself have her own dreams. She held on too closely to Troy, and he probably felt smothered. Who knows? It isn't my business. All I can see is a very sad woman who is holding onto her pride by trying to give me advice that clearly did not work for her.

I manage a tight smile before turning back to Jace. He's noticed my absence and is turned our way, eyes seeking me out. When they lock on me, his shoulders visibly relax. In two long strides he's back at my side, arm around my waist.

"I see you and Stephanie didn't want to talk more football," he comments, oblivious to the tension. He drops a kiss on my cheek.

Before I can answer, Stephanie says, "I thought I'd take Pepper around to meet some of the other girlfriends and wives of the players here tonight. If you join the Stallions, it will be a whole new team for her too."

Jace slips back on his celebrity mask. "I'd like to keep her at my side this evening. I'm sure she'll have opportunities to meet the women soon."

While I'm all about independence and chasing my own ambitions, I'm relieved at this moment that Jace is making a decision on my behalf. Stephanie's weirding me out.

"But Jace, these women will be like her teammates," Stephanie pushes. "Don't you think she should get to know them?"

Jace, like me, is highly suspicious. Stephanie's insistence has him gripping my waist tighter. "Sure. I'll come with."

I want to point out I have my own teammates but I know that's not how she sees it.

She smiles warily before leading us through the crowd toward the bar. "What can I get you to drink?" she asks when we're behind a cluster of others waiting to order. It's a strange question, since it's an open bar and we're perfectly capable of getting our own, but I suppose she's trying to play hostess. As the wife to the star player of the team Jace might join, she must assume this is part of her cheerleading role.

Jace says a beer is fine but I decline anything. I hardly ever drink alcohol anymore with my strict training and competing schedule, and after having one jealous girl spike my drink years ago, I'm not risking it in this environment. Stephanie gazes pointedly at my flat stomach before spinning around and maneuvering herself to the front of the pack to order drinks. Can't a married woman turn down alcohol without an assumption she's pregnant? Sheesh.

Jace and I look at each other and have a silent conversation with our eyebrows and lips twitching. We agree she's a piece of work.

Two women who look vaguely familiar approach us. They are extremely tall and thin and I can only imagine they are models. While cliché, a lot of the players do date and marry models.

"Hiiiii," one of them greets us. "I'm Angel Walker. Tanner's wife." Her eyes move from Jace, to mine. "He's an offensive guard," she explains to me. Her face is open and genuine, and she has kind eyes.

The other woman rocks back on her heels and blushes. "And I'm Leah. Married to Calvin Snyder. Also an offensive guard." Her voice is quiet, and I can't tell if she's shy or crushing on my husband. I'm so used to women flirting with him that it wouldn't surprise me.

"She doesn't know anything about football," Angel explains, pointing a thumb at her friend. "She was dating Cal for months before she even knew what position he played." Her honesty makes us chuckle and Leah blushes harder, shrugging.

"I come to all his games," she protests. "I just don't pay much attention to the actual playing."

Angel scoffs. "Oh, you watch your man, that's for sure. But you don't watch anything else. Don't even know what the score is and you've got some of the best seats in the house. Fo' shame." Angel shakes her head in disapproval.

"It's okay," I reassure Leah. "I've been going to Jace's games since middle school and I still don't understand football. Sometimes it's exciting but most of the time I'm a little bored."

Angel grins at my confession and Leah's eyes widen.

"Really? Bored?" Jace pulls me closer. "You've never told me that before." He's amused, knowing I'll always support him but never be a fanatic.

"Yeah. You guys stop so much and there's all these interruptions. I only like going because your butt looks so good in the uniform."

Jace shakes his head as we all laugh.

"Yeah," Leah says in agreement. "I go for the uniform too."

Stephanie's small frame appears between the two models. "What's so funny?" she asks, sounding annoyed as she hands Jace his beer.

Angel answers, her tone having cooled a notch. "Leah and Pepper only go to the games to watch their men's butts in uniform. Leah here even brings binoculars," Angel outs Leah, who turns a new shade of crimson.

I can see the dynamic between the two, who must be close friends. Angel enjoys embarrassing Leah, who can laugh easily at her own ridiculousness. While the rest of us erupt in laughter at Angel's revelation, Stephanie purses her lips in distaste.

"Pepper, did you even make it to any of the games Jace played at last season?" Stephanie asks. The bitterness dripping from her voice makes me sad for her instead of angry at her implied accusation.

Jace answers for me. "Pep made it to one. I just wish I could have made it to more of her meets. Especially the world cross championships in Switzerland. They don't broadcast all of her races either like they do the NFL. It sucks. Other dudes get to see your cute ass in *your* sweet spandex uniform."

"Don't worry, babe," I say with a pat on his chest. "I've never noticed anyone with binoculars."

"Good. Because I'd hate to miss a game to set any dude straight who's trying to get a close-up of what's mine," he says with a teasing grin before squeezing my butt with one hand and sliding me closer to him.

Leah and Angel giggle. "Aw, so sweet."

I don't bother looking at Stephanie. I know what she would say. After Madeline Brescoll, Wolf and Rex, Savannah Hawkins, and Clayton Dennison, she barely rattles me. Even if her words of "advice" strike disturbingly close to home.

Chapter Three

PEPPER

I hit the roads early the next morning. We were up a little later than usual, but slipped out before most people. While the players are enjoying the off-season, I'm buckling down for the first cycle of what will be the most intense training yet in my career. Jace was still in bed when I snuck out. Usually we wake up together, but I wanted to get a run in before driving up to Brockton. It's never easy leaving a warm Jace in bed when he's in nothing but boxer briefs, but it helps that I have some steam to work off.

Stephanie's words struck a nerve, and they've been festering ever since. I need to run them out of my system. As I wind through the sidewalks toward the bike path, I think about why her little unloading session rattled me. She's simply a bitter woman in a rocky marriage, from what I can tell, and it wasn't so much her words about the cheating or younger women that left a bad taste in my mouth. No, it was that she implied Jace's career matters more than mine. I'm not an Olympian. While I've got collegiate national championships to show off, I've yet to have a major breakthrough professionally. Yes, I placed third, a bronze medal, at the world cross country championships this past fall. But cross country isn't nearly as contested as road races. If I want to make a name for myself outside of my collegiate awards or as

Jace Wilder's wife, then I need to move to the half marathon and marathon distances. I'm on track to make that move, and I shouldn't be in a rush. I graduated less than two years ago.

But I do sense that I need to hit it big to show that my career matters. Sure, I'll probably never make what Jace makes, but that's a matter out of my control. NFL players make more than nearly any athlete in the world, while runners are on the opposite end of the spectrum. That doesn't mean his career has to take precedence all the time. Or does it?

At eight AM on a Saturday morning, the bike path is already busy with cyclists, runners and walkers. It makes it a little difficult to zone out entirely like I can on the trails. I find myself picking up the pace in order to fight the burning in my chest from something entirely unrelated to physical exertion.

Stephanie was right about one thing. Chasing dreams at this level is hard on a marriage. Jace and I are strong. We're solid. We're good. But now I wonder, if one of us has to back off our goals, should that person be me? Is my career less important?

Jace has never made me feel that way. He treats the money he earns like it's ours, like we both earned it together. Still, should I be rearranging my training plan and race schedule in order to support him better?

I suppose these are all thoughts I've wondered before, but Stephanie's warnings brought them to the forefront. She implied I was being selfish, and that hurts. I've never viewed running as selfish before. And now, it's my job. But will my job become being an NFL player's wife if Jace becomes first-string QB? *Should* it?

After an hour and a half on the bike path I make my way back to the hotel. I have another short run this afternoon with Lexi Bell and Sienna Darling, my former college teammates now training in Brockton. As I build up my weekly mileage, I need to run twice a day several times a week.

Even though it's a Saturday, the streets are already busy with traffic, and it takes me a while to get back as I stop at the crosswalks and dodge pedestrians. A lot of the Stallions players live near downtown Denver, with the stadium on the edge of the city. Jace and I haven't talked about where we would live if he got on the team. I hoped he might want to live a little farther north from downtown, closer to Brockton and away from the traffic and hustle and bustle. I don't love running in a city that's so busy, with horns honking and exhaust fueling the air. But then again, maybe it's selfish of me to think about my preferences when my husband is such a superstar. Ugh. I hate that it seems Stephanie did get to me after all, a little bit, if only by opening the door to thoughts I've had in my head all along.

Jace has just woken up when I get back to our suite. I open the bedroom door to find him sitting on the edge of the bed, stretching his arms above his head. His dark hair is tousled, and he has bed sheet creases on his cheek. He turns as I walk toward him, breaking into a lazy grin.

"Morning, gorgeous," he greets me, his voice raspy with sleep. When I slow a few paces away he reaches for me. "Come here."

"I'm all sweaty," I warn him.

He latches a warm hand around my thigh and tugs me to him until I tumble into his lap. "I told you. You're gorgeous no matter what you're wearing. It's all a tease." His hands run over my stomach, my bottom, my legs, as he nuzzles my ear, humming in contentment.

I swing my arms around his neck and peek up into green eyes. His expression is relaxed and peaceful, even with the heat burning behind the heavy lids. This is *my* Jace. Open and gentle. Unguarded. And completely mine.

"Come on," he says as he stands, holding me in his arms like I weigh nothing. "Let's take a shower together."

"Shower?" I question, feeling him hard at my hip and knowing he loves morning sex when we've got the time.

"Just trying to be efficient so we don't keep Buns waiting," he says with a little smirk as he settles me on the counter and turns the shower on. "She left us both text messages this morning with excessive use of emojis."

While Gran's ability to express every emotion through emojis is really quite impressive, sometimes I wish she still had an aversion to texting.

After testing the water temperature, Jace turns back to me, lifting me this time front piggy-back style. "Don't worry, baby, you know I'm great at multi-tasking."

———

When we pull off the highway onto the exit for Brockton, Jace and I both let out happy sighs. We glance at each other and share knowing smiles. It feels good to be home.

Jace takes the familiar roads toward Shadow Lane, but when he pulls onto the street we both grew up on, he doesn't park in his dad's driveway or in front of the apartment building I grew up in with Gran. He pulls into the driveway of an updated ranch home next to his dad's place.

"Why are you parking here?" I ask.

"This place went on the market a couple of months ago and I bought it for Bunny and Wallace. I thought the stairs up to the apartment would start to get tricky for them." Jace says all this while looking at me warily.

I narrow my eyes. "Why are you just telling me this now?" A surge of unwanted and inexplicable anger is threatening to burst out of me.

Jace shifts in the driver seat. "I wanted to surprise you."

"You wanted to surprise me," I repeat, letting doubt fill my voice.

"You were at worlds, and I had to make a decision quickly before someone else made an offer. My dad told me about the house, and I just wanted to do something for Bunny. You know she's been like a gran to me too," he adds, a bit defensively.

"I just can't believe you guys kept this from me. I don't get it."

"We wanted to surprise you. And we didn't want you to stress or worry about the move."

"Did she sell our apartment?" I wonder, a wave of sadness sweeping in.

"No, she's renting it to college students. It's providing extra income for her."

I nod, understanding dawning. We have plenty of money now. By buying Gran a house, she's not only more comfortable, but she has a source of income outside of her pension, from the apartment.

Deciding my anger is unjustified, I lean forward to kiss Jace on the cheek. "Thank you, it's good to be home. Just weird going to a different house."

"Uh, one more thing."

I pause with my hand on the door handle. "Yeah?"

"Lulu moved in with her boyfriend too."

I laugh and shake my head. "This should be fun. Maybe we should stay at your dad's if we want to get any sleep," I muse, imagining the shenanigans that must go down in this place.

We're not disappointed. The front door opens and Gran appears first, arms wide open.

"My babies!" she hollers. "Oh my, I've missed you two." I talk to Gran on the phone almost every day, and exchange numerous text messages now as well, but there's nothing like being held in her arms. She feels a little frailer, not as sturdy as I remember, but smells the same. Like fresh baked bread and the sugar and cinnamon she dumps generously in her coffee.

Jace leans down to hug her next, and his frame seems to envelop her entire body.

A moment later, the rest of the welcome party is surrounding us. Lulu's got orange hair, and I notice she and Gran are wearing matching neon leggings with oversized sweatshirts. They must have the eighties music on again.

Wallace and Lulu's boyfriend Harold strangely fit right in with our little family, and Jim joins a moment later, having heard the commotion from next door.

Jace's phone rings as he's hugging his dad, and he pulls it out of his pocket and ignores the call. As we start to head inside a moment later, it rings again, and Jace sighs. "Sorry guys, it's my agent. Let me just take it so he'll stop calling."

I'm not a huge fan of Drake Vogel. Not only does he have a knack for interrupting my time with Jace, but he gives me the creeps. It's the way he looks at me, the objectifying comments he makes about women in general, and his focus on money over everything else. Yeah, I guess the money thing is his job, but he doesn't have to be so pushy about it.

I have an agent too, Finn Munson, and while the dollar signs aren't as big, Finn and Drake have pretty similar job descriptions. However, Finn seems to actually care about me as a person, my values, my long-term goals personally and professionally.

When I walk inside the house, I realize the inside has been flipped. It was built in the seventies or eighties like everything on this block, but the kitchen and living room are updated.

"Pretty snazzy, huh?" Gran asks with an elbow nudge to my ribs.

"Wow, Gran. I want a tour. This place is sweet." Looking around, I can see that it's filled with the familiar furniture from our old apartment, mixed with some other outdated furniture that must come from Lulu's place or one of the guys'. The same table I ate at for eighteen years is in the kitchen, but there's also a separate dining room with space for maybe a dozen people to sit comfortably.

As I take in the living room opening to a back patio, I notice a dog door just as Dave comes barreling in. He spots me immediately and charges. I'm on my hands and knees getting slobbered all over as I try to contain my giggles long enough to figure out why Dave has a dog door here. When we returned to Ohio last summer for football season, we decided to leave Dave with Jim this time. We were both traveling so much it was hard to give him the attention he needed.

"We connected our back yards," Gran explains. "Made a little door for Dave here so he could see both of us whenever he wanted."

"We would have told you," Jim adds. "But Jace wanted to keep the new house a secret." We'd left Jim in charge of Dave partly because he had a yard, and Gran's apartment didn't. Between the two of them, I bet Dave's spoiled rotten.

When Jace joins me a moment later, I sense something's off before I even look at him. He should be relaxed, happy to give me the surprise of this new house, excited to have Gran show us around. All our favorite foods are piled high on plates and casserole dishes in the kitchen. It should be warmth and comfort settling in around us but instead I feel stiffness and something else coming from Jace as he scratches under Dave's chin.

His jaw flexes when I turn to look at him, and his eyes are distant. "What's up?" I ask.

"I have a few more fundraisers on my schedule than I thought."

My stomach drops. We've both been looking forward to getting into a somewhat regular routine, really *living* together. Yes, we've been married almost three years, but with our schedules, it sometimes feels like we're living separate lives.

"Well, I know you've got one back in Ohio next month. And the car campaign thing in California the month after that. Are there more?"

Jace's chin drops and his eyes close briefly. "Drake says New York wants me at an event next weekend. They heard I was in Denver, and want to reach out, show their interest. I don't know if Denver will take me yet, so I can't close that door." And New York won the Super Bowl. That would be an incredible trade, if Denver didn't work out. But I'd hate New York. Where would I run? Central Park. I've been to a couple races there over the years and the place made my chest squeeze, like I couldn't get enough air. If I thought Denver was too busy and smoggy, New York took it to an entirely different level. But this wasn't about me. Not really.

"Okay. Well, we'll have the week together to get settled in and catch up with everyone."

Jace nods tightly. "Only a few days. I leave on Wednesday. I have to do a photo shoot for Zoran, and Drake figured it'd be best to schedule it when I'm in New York anyway." Zoran's an athletic clothing line that's one of Jace's top sponsors.

The lightness I felt only a moment earlier when we turned onto Shadow Lane floats away, replaced with melancholy. How is it possible to finally be home, but feel so sad and empty at the same time?

Chapter Four

JACE

When Pepper took off for her second run of the day, I knew I needed to work out too. Not because staying in shape was my job. If anything, now was the one time of year I could get away with a day or two off from the gym. No, I needed to work some of my frustration out of my system.

I'd get too much attention if I went to the UC gym, so I headed to Wesley's place, which had a private gym. Wes knew I was back and was expecting me when I pulled up to his house. He had his own place in Brockton now. I hadn't seen it yet, but I'd known by the address that it was nice. It was partway up the foothills, where all the homes had views. The home was modern but it wasn't flashy. Wes was set for life, and he hadn't taken a penny from his parents, as far as I knew. He'd sold a couple of mobile apps early on, while the rest of us were in college, and then used the money he made from those to build an online security program or some shit. I honestly couldn't follow the dude when he got talking in his computer lingo. But I did know he'd sold the program to some guys in Silicon Valley for a shitload of money, so much that Wes didn't have to work again if he didn't want to.

So, he had a home gym and worked out all the time, dabbled in some other computer projects, and was trying to get his new wife pregnant. Zoe Burton – now Zoe Jamison – was teaching fourth grade at the same elementary school we'd all gone to. When no one answered the door I went around back, where I wasn't surprised to find the two lovebirds lounging in a hot tub. The sight of them cozy together made me fucking happy as hell, but also made something inside me twist unpleasantly. They had what Pepper and I couldn't have – time together, relaxing on a Saturday afternoon like normal young couples. A home in the hometown where we wanted to live. Was this what jealousy felt like? The only other time I could recall feeling jealous was when Pepper dated Ryan Harding my senior year of high school. This tightness in my chest was different. It wasn't acute and violent, but more like a longing. I wanted to give this life to Pepper, but it was out of my control. And damn that pissed me off.

Wes hopped out of the tub when he saw me and grabbed a nearby towel.

We grinned like fools at each other before going in for a hug and back slaps. "It's good to see you, bro," he said, eyeing me up and down. "Damn. You got even bigger since Christmas, man."

"For a lazy-ass retiree, you aren't looking so bad yourself," I remarked. Wes was probably in the best shape of his life, from what I could tell. "You look into male modeling, dude? You're cut. And you got that pretty blond hair," I taunted, mostly honestly, as I reached for the lock of hair falling over his forehead.

He batted my hand away. "Fuck off, dude. I'm training for an Ironman this summer. I can probably even run with Pepper sometimes while she's here."

Zoe nudged her husband out of the way and gave me a tight hug. She was one of the only other people in the world who knew that Wesley Jamison was my half-brother, that we shared the same dad. Zoe was my sister-in-law and when they had kids, they'd be my nieces and nephews. Why was I thinking about that shit right now?

I shook my head to snap out of it. Something about being back in our hometown had me all soft.

"This place is unreal, you guys. Nicely done." The huge patio overlooked Brockton below, the view so expansive I could see the football field and the track in the distance.

"We thought we'd throw a little welcome home party for you guys next weekend," Zoe offered.

The knot in my chest tightened. "Shit, sorry Zoe. I have to leave on Wednesday for a few days."

"Oh, bummer," she said, not hiding her disappointment. "Another time."

I punched Wes on the shoulder. "All right, man, show me your weight room. Some of us have to work for a living."

Wes shook his head at my dig but gestured for me to follow him inside, where floor to ceiling windows displayed the view. My dad had used the word "magnificent" to describe Wes's house, and I thought maybe he was drunk because I'd never heard him use that word before and it didn't sound like him at all. But now that I'd gotten a glimpse of inside and outside, I get why Dad expanded his vocabulary to describe it. I was fucking proud of my brother.

Wes gave me a quick tour of the upstairs and main floor before taking me to the basement, where he led me to a huge gym with all the equipment I needed to bust my ass. "This is perfect, man. It's cool if I use this while we're here?"

Wes didn't even bother to answer. "You've got the codes if we're not home. Might want to text first if it's not school hours. We could be naked."

I nodded. "Yeah, I don't need to see that."

As I walked over to connect my iPhone to the stereo and set up some tunes, Wes told me, "You know, there's a place for sale up the road." He might as well be pulling on the knot in my chest with both hands.

I took a deep breath, trying to ease the pressure. "You think they'd rent it for a while?"

"What? No. Don't rent, dude. You can stay here."

I kept my head down as I searched for the right playlist on my phone to plug into the speakers. Fuck, I hated not having a permanent home. Not for me, that wasn't the problem. But for Pepper. She deserved more. "I'll talk to Pepper. We've got space at Bun's but with Lulu there too, she might want to crash here. Or maybe my dad's, so she's closer to Bunny. I don't know. She misses you guys like crazy too. Shit, she'd have everyone in one house if it were up to her."

Wes moved closer to me and I could feel him watching me, studying me. His voice was quiet when he said, "You know as long as she's with you she's good, right? Yeah, she loves the rest of her family and being close to us would be ideal, but as long as you two are good with each other, don't sweat it, man. It'll work out."

I hated it when Wes saw me like he did. Living so far from our family and closest friends, I wasn't used to anyone seeing through me except for Pepper these days. I gave a tight nod before hitting the button to start the playlist. Music blared and I turned to the weight machines.

Wes left me and it wasn't until two, maybe three hours later that I emerged. When I pulled my phone from the speakers, I felt the faint sound of music from above. Making my way up the stairs, I could see at least a dozen people on the pool deck now. Zoe must have decided to invite people over tonight instead of next weekend.

My head was a little clearer, chest a little looser, but I was dripping sweat. I'd jump in the pool if it wasn't still covered for the winter. Instead, I jogged up to the guest room Wes said we could use. After showering in the guest bathroom, I rummaged around in Wes's closet for some jeans and a clean shirt. With no clean boxers, I opted to free-ball rather than borrowing a pair from my brother. Not that I cared, but going commando once in a while felt good.

As I walked outside to the group gathering around a fire pit, the strangest ache hit me. How was it possible to miss my wife when I was with her only hours ago? Would that ever stop?

I saw all familiar faces turn to me when I opened the sliding glass door. They watched me, but not in the celebrity-worship way I'd gotten used to. Okay, sure, there was a little of that too, but these people *knew* me. Yeah, they had a little awe in their eyes from seeing me on TV or whatever, but I could be myself with them. Mostly. I didn't have to put on my celebrity armor and that was a damn relief. It got tiring. I didn't only want Pepper at my side in those moments to keep her away from the assholes, but because I needed her. She gave me the strength to keep up the façade through the public events;

knowing she was there and would be my reward at the end of the night was enough.

Tonight, I wanted her here, but not in that desperate needy way. Because I missed her and I knew she'd want to see everyone, reconnect, revel in the view and gush over Wes and Zoe's place.

Pep's running crew threw hugs my way first. Omar, Rollie, Jenny, Lexi, Brax, and Sienna. A moment later it was my crew from Brockton Public, or the ones still in town at least – Andrea, Remy, Ben, Connor.

We spent a few minutes tossing compliments to each other for the girls, insults between one another for the dudes. Zoe handed me a beer as I spotted a few others flowing in from the side of the house. Just like high school and college, it was impossible to keep a gathering small in this town. My eyes searched the new group for Pepper. As I took a sip of beer, something Wes told me was from a local brewery he invested in, I remembered that Pepper met Lexi and Sienna to run. Brax Hilton and Ryan Harding trained with that same group, though she didn't mention running with them. Still, I couldn't help the dark feelings creeping in as I realized Pepper and Ryan were the only ones from the running group who weren't there right now.

Chapter Five

PEPPER

Running with Lexi and Sienna on my favorite trails is the best feeling ever. They're rooming in a house with Brax, Ryan, and two other guys who run professionally.

"The place is almost as shitty as yellow house," Lexi confesses, referring to the house the guys' cross team lived in in college. "But it works." They're all just scraping by running pro, sometimes picking up hours at the running shop in town to make ends meet. It makes me a little uncomfortable that I don't need to worry about money. Even without Jace in the picture, my sponsorship deals are pretty good. Then again, I probably only got those deals *because* I'm married to Jace and that makes me more interesting. I'm able to avoid thinking about those details when I run solo in Ohio. Technically, I'm on the Newbound Running Team, which trains in Arizona, but I've only joined them for a couple of training blocks. The women on Newbound are mostly better than me with more experience, and don't need any side jobs to make ends meet. At least, no one talked about it when I ran with them.

I thought I would love training with a new group of elite women, but the Newbound dynamic kind of sucks. Monica Herrick, an Olympic marathoner, is the leader of the group, and the main reason most of us joined the team. She's been running professionally for fifteen years and is the protégée of Ray Mintz, the coach of the Newbound team. Unfortunately, Monica is sort of standoffish if not outright mean. She treats the rest of us like competition instead of teammates, which for the most part is true. This isn't college. We might share the same sponsors but we're not *really* teammates. At the end of the day, it's only individual performances that matter in the professional running world. Anyway, I haven't really connected with anyone in the group, which is why I didn't bother joining them for more training sessions in Arizona.

My coach Ray calls as I'm pulling into Gran's driveway.

"Pepper, how was the double today?" he asks.

"Good. I felt strong. I did eight this morning on a bike path, pavement, and ten this afternoon on trails."

"Trails? Like, dirt trails?"

"Yeah. Single track in the mountains. It was pretty hilly. I'll do the tempo run on roads tomorrow."

"I'd stay off the trails whenever possible, Pepper. We really need to get your body ready for the pounding on roads."

I mumble agreement. He's right. As I transition from trail and mountain running to longer distances on the roads, I've got to simulate those races in practice as much as possible. Still, I can't be in Brockton and not sneak in a trail run once in a while.

We chat for a few more minutes about workouts and plans over the next couple of weeks. Ray is based in Arizona with the rest of the team, who train there the majority of the time. It's tricky being coached remotely and requires me to really communicate and analyze my workouts so I can relay where I'm at to Ray. Now that I'm in Brockton with other runners training for a half marathon, I can theoretically do workouts with them. While their paces are close enough to my own, if a little slower, they have a different coach with a different training plan.

"Why so glum, chum?" Gran asks when I walk in the front door.

"I'm not glum. Do I look glum? That's a weird word," I add.

Gran turns from the counter where she's chopping carrots and studies me closer, then pokes me a few times in various parts of my body. "Hmmm. You don't have your usual post-run glow. Are you sure it's normal for you to be getting so toned? I feel like you could use a doughnut. Or five."

I chuckle. "It's my job to be toned. And also to limit the doughnut consumption. But I just got off the phone with my coach in Arizona, and I'm thinking about my workout plan, so maybe I've just got a focused look on my face."

"Maybe. What else is it?" she prods, even as she turns back to the carrots.

I forget what it's like living with Gran. She doesn't miss a thing. "It's just annoying to have a different coach and team while I'm in Brockton. My running friends here are still coached by Ryan's dad, and Ryan actually, he's doing some of the coaching too."

"Can't you just stop being coached by the Arizona guy and join your old teammates?"

Sighing, I snag a carrot and pop it into my mouth before explaining that my sponsorships are tied to the Newbound team, which is connected to the coach. "It's not that I don't like the coach. He's good. Ray Mintz is considered the best marathon coach in the country. And the girls on Newbound are some of the best distance road runners in the country too. I really don't have any reason to complain."

"Our girl's homesick, that's what I think," Lulu declares as she joins us in the kitchen. "We doing chicken noodle tonight?"

"Sure thing," Gran says. "*My* recipe."

"We've had to do a few blind taste tests on our fav dishes," Lulu explains with an eyeroll. "Bunny here won on the chicken soup but my lasagna is still the top pick."

"Who got to do the tasting?" I would not want to be in that role. I can only imagine Lulu and Gran watching, one hand on a hip with a threatening kitchen knife held in the other. I shudder.

"Wallace, Harold, and Jim," Lulu says as she starts peeling an onion.

"So, Lulu," Gran says, "how is it you think our girl is homesick if she's home now?"

"'Cause she's being pulled in a bunch of directions. She ain't settled."

It's true, but there's no solution. My contract keeps me with

Newbound until June at the earliest. I can always join the Brockton team then and figure out the sponsorship situation, but it all depends on where Jace lands.

"If Jace doesn't end up on the Stallions," Gran muses, "why would you stay with the Arizona team? Why not just join the Brockton team if you're going to be coached remotely anyway?"

"It's complicated, Gran. It's not that simple. I was really lucky to get on Newbound. They're the best distance runners in the country, the best coach, the best sponsorships. I can only justify leaving them if we're in Brockton to stay. It'd be nuts to ditch them only to be coached remotely by someone else." And that someone else might be Ryan, which would be even weirder.

"Well, you know I'm all for being nuts," Gran says with a wink tossed my way.

"Damn straight," Lulu adds with a nod. Her orange hair sticks out as if she's been electrocuted, but somehow, it suits her.

Loving their familiar antics, my spirits lift a little as I find the bathroom to shower. It's not until I'm in my towel, deciding what to wear, that I realize Jace should be back by now. Finding my phone, I discover over a dozen messages. A couple from Jace, Zoe, and my other friends in Brockton. News has spread we're back in town, and everyone is gathering at Wes and Zoe's new place.

I borrow Gran's car and as I wind up the road, passing Remy Laroche's parents' house, I'm in awe that Wes and Zoe live up here. It's not only that they've had financial success, it's what they chose to do with that money. They could have traveled the world, bought a penthouse in Manhattan or something, but instead they got a house they plan to live in maybe forever, in their hometown where Zoe can keep teaching if she wants. Zoe told me the house is big enough for them to "grow into" and have lots of kids. They actually thought about whether the place was kid-friendly when they bought it. It's just all so mature and grown up.

I spot the expansive driveway, now so filled with cars that there are several parked along the side of the road. Pulling in behind one, I shake my head. Sure, my closest friends might be all grown up now, but some things never change. I bet they have a keg and beer pong set up too.

Following the noise to the side door leading to the back yard, memories of other Brockton parties hit me. Somehow, it's only the good moments that stand out, though I know if I think about it for too long I'll recall Madeline Brescoll dumping a drink on me, Wolfe dragging me to a pool house... yeah, better to focus on the happy times.

"Pepper!" A familiar voice calls my name and I spin around to find Ryan jogging my way, a big grin on his face.

"Hey Ryan! So good to see you." I open my arms for a hug when he reaches me. I've run into him a few times in Brockton and at a couple of races since I graduated. It's now been over seven years since we briefly dated each other, and while I haven't forgotten, it feels too far in the past to be relevant. He seems to be on the same page, and we treat each other like any old friends or teammates.

I'm hugging like this, soaking in the comfort and nostalgia, when I hear Jace's voice.

"Pepper. Ryan." I think he means for it to sound like a greeting, but I detect the tension beneath it.

Of course, his voice causes us to break apart quickly, as if we really were sharing an inappropriate moment.

Ryan greets Jace awkwardly before we all join the others on the pool deck.

I lean into Jace and squeeze his hand, urging him to look at me. I thought these insecurities were behind us, but maybe they never will be. After all, Ryan is my only ex-boyfriend. Still, I wish Jace would get over it already since Ryan's going to be around, maybe *forever*, if I train with his group. Jace's jaw clenches as his eyes meet mine. No, it's not insecurity causing him to react like this. There's something darker going on. We're too solid, too confident in each other, to get upset over a little jealousy. We trust each other. So why does Jace look like he wants to punch something?

I want to pull him away and talk it out but we're the center of attention. It's not only our close friends here, but from what I can tell, most of the people we know from Brockton who stayed in town have shown up. Brockton is the kind of place that people aren't looking to leave. I've met people who are dying to get out of their hometown, but I've never met anyone in Brockton like that. Some leave for college and end up elsewhere for jobs or relationships, but most come back or never leave in the first place.

After nearly an hour being bombarded with questions about football and running, Jace pulls me close to ask if I got dinner.

"No. I'm starving," I admit. He loves taking care of me and pounces on this opportunity. I can tell just by starting the grill and getting Wesley and Zoe on board with grilling, Jace is feeling better. Managing to break away, I circle my arms around him as he flips burgers.

"You okay?" I ask quietly, rising on my tiptoes to reach his ear.

He puts down the spatula and turns around, resting his hands low on my hips. "Now that you're here I am. I want to hear about your run. Good to be back?"

I know what he really wants to ask; I also know he's trying not to ask it, so I spare him the struggle. "I literally just saw Ryan for the first time when I got here. Yeah, I'll be running with him sometimes but you know he's moved on, Jace. It was a long time ago."

Jace lowers his forehead to mine. "I know. It's not even him. It's what he represents."

"What he represents?"

Jace pulls back a little, jaw set. He doesn't want to elaborate and is about to turn around to reach for the spatula but I tug him tighter to me. Nope. We aren't doing this non-sharing thing. There can be no emotion-suppressing in this marriage. It's been too destructive for us in the past. "What does he represent, Jace?" I push.

He knows it too, though I can tell it takes effort to force it out. He's practically gritting his teeth when he admits, "The things I can't give you."

His words surprise me enough that I loosen my hold and blink a few times, trying to process. He's already back to the burgers, and we're surrounded by people again, before I can follow up with more questions. *The things he can't give me?*

When it hits me what he's getting at, I wonder why I was even confused in the first place. Home. Brockton. That whole "being settled" thing Gran and Lulu were getting at. But that's all so minor compared to Jace Wilder himself. I've got the guy I've loved my entire life right here at my side. I'd rather live with him in New York City or Ohio or wherever we land than be without him here in Brockton. Doesn't he know that?

Chapter Six

PEPPER

Of course, as the weeks go on, and Jace continues to be called at the last minute to fly somewhere for a campaign, a fundraiser, a publicity event, whatever, I start to wonder if I really do have him. Yeah, I've got his heart, his loyalty, his trust, all of that, but without his physical presence, it feels empty.

"You miss him, don't you?" Zoe asks.

Despite Ray's advice, I'm getting in one of my easy runs on the trails with Zoe and Dave. Poor Dave rarely gets to run with me now that I've got my strict running plans.

"So much, Zoe. Is that weird?"

"Why would that be weird? He's your husband."

Zoe's not running professionally but she's actually in great shape. She's helping Wes train for an Ironman and runs a lot with him. Given that I'm ramping up to a hundred miles a week, I'm impressed that she's easily keeping up with me and holding a conversation. Sure, it's an easy run, but I've learned that my slow pace is getting too fast for some of my running friends who don't compete anymore.

"I don't know. We have the rest of our lives together. I do talk to him every day, even if I don't see him in person every day. I know everything that's going on in his life, and he knows everything in mine. We're as close as two people can be."

"But you still miss him," she finishes for me.

Knowing she gets it, understands it, that helps me feel like I'm not totally crazy. "Yeah. I think that if I knew this was only for a short while and we just had to get through a few more months, that'd be better. But this is our lives."

"If he lands in Denver, it will be better," Zoe encourages.

"It would definitely be better if he trades to the Stallions," I concede, even knowing that's far from a sure thing. "He can try to do more promotional stuff locally that way too."

It would actually be *a lot* better if he landed with the Stallions, but I can't get my hopes up.

"I see why it's rough, Pep. When I was at Mountain West and Wes was at Princeton, I always questioned what we were doing. I didn't know how we'd know if we were meant to stay together forever if we weren't even in the same place for more than a few weeks at a time. But it was also easier than what you're going through, because I knew that eventually we *would* be, and if we could make it until that time, it'd be worth it."

"Yeah, the only end in sight for us is when we both retire," I say with a humorless chuckle.

"You'll never retire from competing, Pep," Zoe says, and I think she's teasing until she adds, "It's just part of you. You wouldn't be you without it."

"You really think that?"

"Hell yeah. I know plenty of runners and athletes. But no one like you. From that first day I dragged you to practice in your high top Converse, it was like love at first hill sprint."

Talk turns to running, my switch from trails and mountain races to the longer distances on the road, the build-up to the marathon. The marathon is the ultimate race for a distance runner, the most followed and contentious distance in the world. Not everyone's bodies can handle running marathons, competing in them, for more than a season or two. I've finally found a solid balance in my training where I push hard, but I know when I'm getting too close to the edge of injury. I'm doing enough strength training now that I'm strong all around, able to withstand the increase in mileage. Still, it's a little risky making the move to the marathon this early in my career. Most distance runners wait until they've hit some milestones on the track in the 5K or 10K.

I explain all this to Zoe and she asks, "So why do it now? Are you feeling pressured from being on a team with so many elite marathoners?"

"No. It wasn't my coach's idea. Actually, he resisted it at first when I mentioned it." I've explained it to Jace, who understood where I was coming from, but it's different with Zoe. She doesn't have whatever Jace and I have that makes us want to chase the biggest, craziest goals. Not that she's a slacker or anything, she's just normal, reasonable. Jace and I aren't normal or always reasonable when it comes to our passions. But I try my best to explain it. "I need to prove myself. Which," I quickly justify my words, "I know sounds silly. I've got a lot of great accomplishments under my belt." I start to continue but she interrupts me.

"Don't worry, Pep. I'm with you. Yes, you got national titles in high school, and college, and you just hit the podium at the world cross championships. But the marathon is the biggest stage and you want to conquer it too. And you especially want it because you want to stand on your own two feet. Prove you deserve your sponsorships. That you aren't in Jace's shadow."

I suck in a breath at her last statement, and it's not from exertion as we wind up a hill. No, it's because everything she said was spot on. Even the last part. The one part I didn't talk to Jace about. Yes, I want to prove myself in the elite professional field. But it's more than that.

"I know that's messed up. It's not like I'm competitive with Jace himself, or need or want the spotlight." I think about it, trying to articulate why it matters. "It's just that being married to an NFL quarterback, it's easy to question your own self-worth. Or not self-worth exactly. My purpose. Like, most of the wives don't have their own goals. It's just to support their husbands' dreams and follow them around. Which I'm not bashing. Not at all. Sometimes that's how it needs to be done. It's what makes sense."

"But not for you and Jace," Zoe says with such confidence, I feel a wave of tension leave my body. She gets it. She so gets it.

"No. That's not us. Neither of us would want that."

"You know, the imbalance thing, it's at a higher level for you two since it's your dreams and passions, but Wes and I deal with that somewhat too."

"Because he made so much money so quickly?" I hadn't really thought about that. Zoe has never mentioned that the money was a source of tension in their marriage.

"That's part of it, but it's always changing. Like, I don't need to work because of the money, but I do, for now at least. Maybe that will change when we have kids, but it's like you said, finding your purpose or whatever, your role. It's partly what I need but what Wes needs too. Me having a job, a normal one with normal hours that gives me a community and goals and everything, that's good for both of us. I think Wes is still figuring it out. He was a little lost when he realized he really didn't *need* to work anymore. He still tinkers around with stuff on his computer so I guess he *is* working, but he doesn't have any goals."

"That's why he's training for an Ironman?"

"Yep."

"He gets restless quick. Maybe you should try for triplets. That will make it real clear what his purpose and role are."

Zoe laughs. "We're trying. I know we're young, but we both want a lot of kids. Wes because he was an only child and wanted siblings, me because I have a ton of siblings and need a certain level of chaos in a house to feel like home."

"I can't wait."

"We've already picked out names for like ten theoretical kids. What about you guys? I know you have a lot going on but do you talk about it?"

"Nope." I admit this easily at first, but then feel a little sadness. "Maybe we're just too caught up in our own dreams and goals right now to think about that."

"There's nothing wrong with that, Pep. Stop being so hard on yourself."

Am I being hard on myself? Maybe. Kids seem like a given, but someday, way in the future. My mind thinks in cycles: get through this training cycle, Jace's season, another training cycle, Olympic Trials, maybe Olympics, repeat. That's how my life is right now, in blocks of time that I can manage.

———

I fly out the next morning for a race in Boston, excited to have Jace all to myself while he watches me race for the first time in what feels like forever. He's meeting me there, flying from New York where he attended another event with the team there. But as I'm waiting to board the plane he calls to tell me that his agent booked an advertising campaign for him the next day and he can't come to Boston after all.

"If you tell me to blow it off and come see you, I'll do it in a heart-beat," he offers. I can't tell if he *wants* me to do this, or if he's just trying to make it better. But we decided early on that we wouldn't get in the way of each other's careers, force each other to decide. All these ad opportunities are new and he can't be turning them down just as his career is taking off.

"I'm not going to do that, Jace. This isn't a big race. If I make the Olympics someday I expect you to be there, but this is just a 10K road race. I've done plenty of 10Ks in my life. It's not a big deal." He also knows I'm just trying to make it better. The truth is, this race is my debut into the elite road racing circuit. After racing only on the trails or track since graduating nearly two years ago, I've yet to race at a highly competitive road 10K like this one. There will be lots of former Olympians from all over the world and in the running world at least, there's been a lot of buzz about where I'll stand.

Jace changes the subject as I hear them call my boarding group. "Frankie and Lizzie are gonna come up for a few days when we get back on Monday." He sounds as torn as I feel. We love spending time with our friends but how is it possible to be married to someone and have so little alone time with them?

"I miss you," I say quietly. It slips out, and I can practically feel

Jace's frustration and sadness in the small sigh he makes on the other end.

"God, baby, I miss you so bad. It's starting to actually hurt. Do you feel it?"

I didn't know he was feeling it as hard as I did. How could I when I see him a few days a month now and during that time one of us is training or in some sort of meeting?

"Yeah. I do." My fist goes to my chest, right where that ache is, but it's not like he can see me. I want to ask how the trade negotiations are going, if all this travel and effort is helping his cause. If there's any leeway with the Stallions. It seems like his agent has him traveling to New York and California more often than Jace is in Denver, except I don't really know how this all works.

I don't ask. It's too important. It matters too much. I don't want to know if the answer is one I won't like.

"I have to board," I say, my voice a little hoarse from an emotion I can only identify as sadness.

"Okay." He hesitates, and I wonder if he wants me to beg him to ditch his commitments in New York to meet me in Boston. But instead he says, "I love you. Be safe." And we hang up.

Chapter Seven

PEPPER

Damn it feels good to race. As we pass the final mile marker and head into the last stretch, I know I'm doing exactly what I'm meant to do. Like Zoe said, this is a part of me. The drive to compete. When I embrace it, I'm alive. The only other thing that makes me feel this alive is being with Jace, but I push that thought away. Even as my muscles start to burn and spectators scream from the side of the road, I'm missing him.

I settled in with the lead pack from the beginning. Two runners from Kenya broke off at mile three and are likely too far ahead to reach. The prize money is big, and because of that, the field is deep. The restlessness in the pack grows when the finish line comes into view with half a mile to go. We all want to be on that podium. Not just for the huge paycheck, but the prestige, the momentum going into the rest of the season. We want the podium finish for all the practical reasons required for our jobs as runners, yes, but mostly for the pure raw competitiveness that has us out here, lungs burning, in the first place.

A few runners keep trying to pull away, make a break for it, but aren't able to get far from the pack before we reel them back in. As we barrel closer to the finish, Monica Herrick bursts ahead, and instinct has my legs trigger to pick up the pace with her. I was about to make my own move, and I'm ready for the surge. I've worked on my speed, and I'm able to turn over my legs faster and take it to the next level. I don't feel anyone with us, and as I dig inside me, sprinting ahead, I sense Monica falling back too. I'm gaining on the two Kenyan runners who are out of reach. The sound of the crowd grows, and when they break the tape right next to each other, I'm only steps behind.

My time of 32:14 is my fastest 10K time ever, a feat given how often I've raced this distance on the track, which is generally faster than a road race. And the best part is that I feel great. Like the season, this journey of road racing and building toward the marathon and the Olympics has only just begun.

Lexi and Sienna finish a minute or two after me. While Monica and a couple other Newbound teammates are here, it's my old college teammates I find myself drawn to, whom I end up cooling down with after watching the men's race end.

Ryan hits the podium in a third-place finish as well, the first American man. I know this is big for me. Beating Monica Herrick, hell, beating all the other Americans and most of the foreign runners in the field today, is a huge statement of where I'm at. A lot of the top cross runners and mountain runners ended up in those races because they couldn't quite hang with the top field on the roads, where the bigger money and sponsorships are. But I've shown that's not me. I'm not only in the pack, I came out on top of it today.

I savor the feelings of racing well, grateful for my health and solid training. I know these races don't come together every time, and I've got to soak it in when they do. After warming down, I smile on the podium for pictures, and then take a few with Ryan for the media, who want the two American podium finishers together. It reminds me a little of our high school days. I want to laugh with him about how he was there for my very first plane flight to Nationals, but bringing up the time when we were dating seems inappropriate. It's amazing that I fly nearly every month now for a race.

I don't know how it's possible to be on top of the world and still have that ache in my chest, but I do.

When I get on the plane the next morning to fly home, I should be feeling excitement that the ache will get some relief. Jace will be meeting me at the airport. But as soon as I open my email while waiting for the plane to board, a new sensation hits. One that's not so familiar. Anger.

Chapter Eight
JACE

I could feel a few eyes on me as I stood behind the black rope things with others waiting for people coming off the escalators from flights. The baseball cap over my head didn't do much for disguise. While I could fly under the radar in New York a little better, I was somehow more recognizable in Colorado. Maybe it was because more people knew of me around here, or maybe there were so many celebrities in New York no one paid much attention, but I was getting restless. Someone was about to say something, which would open me up as fair game and I'd be swarmed in a few minutes. I didn't want that. I was contemplating going back to wait at my Jeep, which was parked in the closest lot. There were definitely little perks to having an NFL paycheck, like not thinking about paying an outrageous amount for convenient airport parking.

But then I saw her. It was always like this when I saw Pepper in a crowd. Not even a crowd. Just, anywhere. Especially when it had been over a week since I'd last touched her. She was so damn bright. Like a glow of light around her, some sort of angel. I knew that kind of shit was supposed to wear off. Seeing her through this lens, the one where she was just it for me, my peace my calm my everything, it had only grown more into focus over the years. Sure, there were pretty women everywhere, but Pepper was the only one who shone like this for me.

So despite the annoyance and a little anger I had brewing from the photos my agent sent me earlier, my heart fucking soared as she walked off the escalator, looking around. I'd texted where I'd be, and she tugged on her backpack straps as her eyes roamed over the people waiting.

She spotted me quickly and when our eyes locked, I was surprised I didn't get the easy smile she usually gave me. This one was tight, hard, hurt. Fuck. My heart rate picked up and I wanted to shove the people in front of me to the side and jump over the rope.

Instead, I maneuvered around them to meet her and she fell into my arms. Her body felt right there, against my chest. She still wanted my comfort, no matter what was going on in her head. I held her tight for a minute, but couldn't get enough of her with that backpack on. Slipping it off over her shoulders, I put it on my own.

"You been waiting long?" she asked.

"Nope. Got in twenty minutes before you. Dropped my bag in the car and when I got back, you'd landed." I tried to search her eyes, but we both noticed the people around us watching, starting to talk about who we were, so I took her hand instead.

When we got to the Jeep a minute later, I was ready to explode. From wanting to touch her, and wanting to know why she was withdrawn.

"What's going on, baby?" She'd just had an amazing race, so I knew it wasn't that.

She shook her head tightly and swallowed. "You..." she started and stopped, swallowing again. I was watching the column of her throat as she swallowed and didn't realize the tear leaking from her eye until she started talking. "You were with Madeline Brescoll."

My eyebrows drew together. "What are you talking about?"

She turned to look at me. "I know that we've had photos fuck with us before, that they don't always tell the truth. But this one was in the New York Times, so I'm thinking it's not fake."

How did I not know what she was talking about? Drake was usually on the ball about alerting me to anything unusual in the media, anything that could be problematic.

"My agent sent it to me," she said. "The two of you together at some charity event on Saturday night." She lowered her eyes, looking at her hands. "Look, I know you have to go to those things. I know you might not have wanted to take a photo with her. But you two looked real cozy, arms around each other. She was way too close. God, I've never wanted to claw someone's eyes out like I wanted to when I saw how smug she looked. How could you let her get that close?"

I pushed my seat all the way back, unbuckled her seat belt, and hauled her over to me. She let me, and slid her legs easily on either side of my hips. We needed to be connected. "Better already, right?" I asked, trying to ease the hurt I could feel weighing her down.

"Why didn't you tell me you saw her? What happened?"

"I didn't say anything because you were racing the next morning. I only spoke to you briefly before your race and then after. I probably would have brought it up this week but wasn't sure. I didn't think it mattered. Didn't want to bring up someone who doesn't deserve to get in the middle of us, when we only get so much time together."

She shifted on my lap as I felt some of the tension drift out of her body. My hand roamed the bare skin under her tee shirt, dipped below the waistband of her jeans. I needed to feel her skin.

I told Pepper all there was to tell. "I didn't know she'd be at this charity. Didn't even know she was in New York. Actually, I don't know much of anything about her or why she was there. We barely spoke."

"How'd you end up in the picture?"

"I guess she knows Drake, who was there too. She knew I didn't want to talk to her, but then Drake got all excited we were from the same town and knew each other in high school. I wasn't about to cause a scene and be an asshole so when he called over some photographers, I just went with it. I don't know why or how that shit ended up in the New York Times. If I'd known that I would've been a dick and walked away. I just didn't want it to cause anyone to sniff around looking for a story, so I went along with it."

Because we both knew there *was* a story. Several actually.

"It was in the New York Times because she's gorgeous," Pepper stated like it was obvious. "And she's the daughter of the biggest brewery owner in the nation, a socialite. She was there representing Brescoll Brewery, the main supporter of this charity, the host for the event. You didn't know all that?"

"Not until I got there. I knew what the charity was but it was a last-minute thing Drake lined up. I didn't get into the details or who was the driving force or anything. How'd you know all that?"

"It was in the article."

We sat there for a moment, faces inches apart, bodies pressed close. We knew nothing could come between us. But we just kept getting hit, and even as we learned to put it all out there, talk it out, it didn't mean we didn't feel the blows. If I could go back and never touch Madeline Brescoll I'd do it in a heartbeat. But that wasn't an option. My nostrils flared as I tried to push down the anger at my past, at the things I couldn't control.

"Drake should've said something," I said, a realization dawning.

"Maybe he felt guilty he had them take the photo in the first place and was hoping we wouldn't see it."

I shook my head. No. That wasn't it. Whether we liked it or not, Pepper and I had risen to become a popular couple in the media. We were young, both athletes gaining momentum in our careers. People liked that shit. But Drake didn't see it that way. He saw my married status as a barrier to the bachelor image, which he thought would get me more attention, bigger sponsors.

"No. Drake set this up. He knew that a photo of me with her would stir shit up, get people talking. That's all he wants to do. Keep me in the limelight, good or bad."

"It doesn't stir shit between *us* though, okay?" Pepper lowered her chin to look at me closely, her voice gentle as she swayed a finger between us. "I'm not mad at you. I trust you. It hurt to see that photo. She's not someone I ever want to think about, especially not with you. But I understand how it happened. I'll always ask before jumping to conclusions. All that shit she threw at us when we were a new couple, we got through that. We can get through whatever comes next."

I loved this woman. With her reassurances, the hardness straining in my jeans pulsed and Pepper let out a little moan as she pressed into it. I wasn't trying to start anything, but my body couldn't help it with my wife so close, even if we were talking about some shitty stuff.

I still had to ask her about the photo with Ryan, but it was taking all my willpower not to kiss her. If I did, I wouldn't be able to stop. And I couldn't take her in the Jeep. Not here. Talk about a story for the media if security came knocking on the Jeep for rocking back and forth in the parking lot.

I steadied her hips, holding her firmly. "You know there's a picture of you and Ryan floating around the internet from yesterday's race, right? Drake didn't have any problem sending *that* one to me."

"Yeah, but only because we both hit the podium and were the first Americans."

I shook my head. "I know." It still sucked. It still made me furious to see his arm thrown around my wife, their happy matching grins and postrace glows. He was there at the race when I couldn't be. When I was stuck at some event where I knew no one. Except for my scheming agent and Madeline Brescoll. I was more mad at myself than with her.

"You know Drake might not really have tried to stir shit. It was probably unintentional. It's not like he knows about your history with her," Pepper said with a frown.

"You know better than anyone I've gotta be careful who I trust. And I don't trust this guy. He doesn't respect us. Our marriage. He's made enough comments it's clear we're not on the same page. But I need him right now, and playing along with being in the public eye will benefit me in negotiating a trade. As soon as the trade is done I'm gonna start talking to Frankie's agent."

"You don't think we're being overly suspicious because of our past?"

I raised my eyebrows. "Pep, I know it's in your nature to think the best of people. To want to give them the benefit of the doubt. And you trying to stick up for Drake is real cute when I know you don't like the guy. And not just because he's the one causing me to travel all the time, but because your instincts tell you he's not good people."

She dropped her shoulders and sank into me further, resting her head on my shoulder. "Can we get out of here and just be together? I need you so bad, without any of this bullshit."

Hearing curses from Pepper's mouth meant business. "I know we have three potential houses in Brockton right now, baby," I told her as I situated her back in the passenger seat and buckled her in, "but none of them are really ours. As much as I love everyone, I need you alone and naked and I'm not waiting until everyone gets a chance to see us first."

"What do you have in mind?" she asked, her voice a little breathy.

I glanced over to find her squirming in her seat. "No hotel. Someone might recognize us and I'm too impatient to check in."

"You know I've never required a bed," Pepper said.

"That's my girl."

I headed to the closest campsite I could think of on my way to Brockton. It was April, which meant it hadn't yet opened for the season. But wasn't inaccessible. It was perfect. With all the shit going on around us, all it took was the two of us together, skin on skin, no one to interrupt, and the restlessness in me faded away. As long as I could have this, always, I was good.

Chapter Nine

PEPPER

It's a good thing we stopped at the campsite on the way up or we wouldn't have had any alone time. When we pull up to Gran's house, Frankie and Lizzie have beaten us. Jace and I are both feeling lighter with the physical connection reestablished. We still have stuff to deal with, but it's nothing we can't handle. I didn't get a chance to mention to Jace that my agent sent me the New York Times article because he'd gotten questions about our relationship. My agent implied the media might run with the two photos of each of us with different people, and our exes at that.

It didn't bother me though. Not now that I'd had Jace inside me, had his hand in mine now, and we were back in Brockton together. Nothing could get to me right now.

Frankie is one of many of my friends Gran has taken under her wing. Growing up, Gran treated all my friends like family. It didn't change in college, especially with so many of my teammates far from their own families. She cooked, baked, knitted, cheered, and hung out with my friends like they were her own grandkids. As one of Jace's best friends, Frankie got the Gran treatment too. He's obviously soaking it in when we get in the house.

Frankie sits at the kitchen table with a plate of food piled so high it looks like it might topple over. Lizzie is next to him with a slightly more reasonable amount of food on her plate, but I can see Gran trying to scoop out more from the dish on the table.

I don't bother asking why they're eating dinner mid-afternoon. I can smell the lingering scent of pot in the air, and know Gran loves to cook and feed people when she's high. Also, when she's not high.

With Jace gone so much, we decided to make the spare room at Gran's place home base. I don't want to be without him at Wes and Zoe's place or at his dad's. I'm more comfortable at Gran's house, even surrounded by four people in their seventies who have the tendency to act like they're twenty when the mood suits.

After hugging our friends, we settle into the other seats, knowing Gran's going to feed us whether we want it or not. It's an eclectic meal: chicken pot pie, banana bread, potato chips, and roasted vegetables. I'm guessing Lulu got involved.

"How long have you guys been waiting on us?" I ask, letting Gran pile my plate because I know it makes her happy.

Lizzie rolls her eyes. "Frankie wanted to leave first thing in the morning but I reminded him you guys wouldn't even land until late morning."

"I did a workout, then headed up. Got here a couple hours ago," Frankie says. "I get restless in the off-season." He shrugs before shoving another forkful of food in his mouth.

"He wants me to quit my job so I can entertain him all day," Lizzie explains with mock annoyance. She has a customer service job that she hates, so I could see her actually taking that offer once they get married.

"Man, I know you're not trying to make a trade this off-season, but you've got tons of sponsorships. Don't you have to travel for campaigns and shit for them? You really get bored in the off-season?" Jace asks.

"Hell yeah. I miss competing and training with the team. I go to charity functions every once in a while, but rarely travel for them. I've only had to travel once for one of my sponsors."

"How the fuck – sorry, Buns – how'd you pull that off?"

Frankie shrugs his big shoulders again. "Made it clear to my agent I wanted to keep travel to a minimum. I got my family in Kansas to visit in the off-season, my girl with a nine to five job I want to see. Besides, I don't want to burn out from travel and shit by the time the season starts. Told my agent to work it out. She probably turns down a few opportunities for me, but I'd rather not know the details. Keeps it simple. I trust her."

Jace and I look at each other. "You need this agent," I state the obvious.

Jace shakes his head. "I tell my agent to minimize travel on practically a daily basis and that fucker keeps telling me this is the life I chose and to suck it up and stop whining. I knew he was a dick, but I'm seeing he's more of one that I even thought."

Gran smacks Jace in the back of his head, scolding him for bad language at the dinner table. She doesn't usually mind but we're supposed to be better behaved at this table for some reason.

We chat more about agents, the requirements of sponsors for other players, realistic expectations for travel and obligations. Gran bustles around us and the kitchen, reveling in this opportunity to take care of us. Lulu, Harold, and Wallace left earlier for something going on at the assisted living facility that the guys were staying at before they met Lulu and Bunny. While I know Gran wants her independent living situation as long as possible, I love knowing she'll be perfectly happy at an assisted living place if it ever comes to that someday. She's already a social butterfly over there just because she likes the community.

I'm glad I managed to get in a quick run before my flight this morning. The day after a race, even a shorter one early in the season, my training is minimal. It means I've got the rest of the day off. After nearly two hours sitting around chatting, we send Gran off to join her regular Bingo obligations with the others, and we head over to Wes and Zoe's place.

They've got a huge table in a dining room they never use, and I can't help jumping up and down when I find a few puzzle boxes sitting in the middle of it. "Yes!" I pump a hand in the air. Jace and I love doing puzzles together but it feels like forever since we've sat down and tackled one.

Jace's knowing smile at my enthusiasm tells me he's the one who had this idea.

"I didn't know what to get so I got a bunch," Wes says with a gesture to the pile of puzzles. He never was as into the puzzles as me and Jace. He just went along with us.

"Some of these say ages seven to twelve, Wes," Jace says with raised eyebrows, holding up one of the boxes.

"Yeah, those are for me," Wes says with a sigh.

Frankie and Lizzie look confused. Jace just shakes his head. "For a dude who can build multi-million-dollar computer security programs, you really suck at puzzles."

Zoe defends her husband. "Guys, those ones that say ages seven to twelve are seriously hard. Especially if you're drinking," she adds, taking a sip of wine. "Besides, I have to go to bed in like two hours. Some of us have to wake up early for school. Did you guys even know how early the teachers had to get up when we were kids? Shit. I never thought about it until I became one but it's way too early."

We settle in at the table, Jace and I working on one of the bigger ones, Zoe and Wes on one of the kiddie ones, and Frankie and Lizzie helping out here and there, laughing at our antics.

"So Frankie," Zoe asks, "is this a normal night for a Stallions player? I mean we've got these two NFL players on their off-season. I know Jace and Pepper here aren't normal. You think puzzling it up with the wifeys is what the other Stallions are doing?"

Frankie chuckles. Lizzie scoffs. "Actually," she says, "Calvin Snyder and his wife Leah are closet nerds. She was a Victoria's Secret model but the two of them are super into chess. I bet they spend the off-season battling each other at chess all day."

"Oh yeah, we met Leah at Frankie's event. I liked her." Can't really picture the bombshell from that night nerding out with pawns and rooks but she and her friend seemed cool.

"Hey, they're having a few of us over to their place this weekend," Frankie says. "Leah and Calvin. You guys should all come. Get to know some people on the team outside of a publicity thing. I think only Angel and Tanner are coming."

"Sounds kind of small. You sure they'd want you inviting all us ragers?" I ask.

"Nah. As long as it's cool people and no drama they'll be down."

"Good thing we can't go," Wes says. "'Cause Zoe always brings the drama."

We all know he's joking but Zoe smacks him lightly on the cheek in mock outrage. "Ski trip we planned a while ago. We would invite you guys but you know with that professional athlete thing we figured you wouldn't be able to enjoy the slopes."

I've had two glasses of wine, which is pretty unusual for me, and it's making the words flow out of me. "Okay, so I liked Angel and Leah. But Stephanie Bremer got all up in my business. She also basically said that all the guys on the team cheat on their wives. What's up with that?"

Lizzie and Frankie share a look. There's a long pause and I glance at Jace, who opens his mouth to speak, but Frankie starts responding. "Troy Bremer does. I know he's got the family image, All-American guy thing going on in the media but he's actually an asshole on and off the field. Takes a ton of PR to keep that image up. Dude better retire before the truth comes out about him."

Lizzie sighs. "It's not like he's the only asshole on the team. It doesn't help he's the leader." She looks pointedly at Jace. "Believe me, I'm hoping you'll take his spot for a lot more reasons than having you guys around to hang out with."

Zoe says, "It's still weird to me that Jace Wilder, the bad boy from high school, is going to be the role model for husbands and men across the country." She shakes her head.

I laugh. "I wouldn't go that far." Well, it's not that much of a reach. Scary.

"So are most of the women on the team like you, Leah and Angel or are they more like Stephanie?" I'm more interested in the women I'll be dealing with than the asshole behavior of the men on the team.

Lizzie shakes her head. "There are three types of women with the Stallion players. The ones like Stephanie, whose husbands cheat and who are real bitter about it." She holds up one finger and then a second. "Then there are the ones whose husbands cheat but they don't care because they knew what they were signing up for. They know they're trophy wives and their reward is the money and the lifestyle and they play along." She raises a third finger before declaring, "And then there are people like us, with husbands or boyfriends who don't cheat and who try to keep lives and relationships as normal as possible despite the money and lifestyle."

We all stare at Lizzie for a minute or two, taking this in, thinking it over. "Yeah," I finally say, breaking the silence. "That actually makes sense. I didn't spend much time with the women on the Browns team, but from what I saw, it was similar."

Jace pulls me over to him, hauling me onto his lap. He always seeks as much physical contact with me as possible. "You don't seem fazed by the reality that most of the guys on the team aren't loyal to their wives or girlfriends. That should bother you more."

He's talking just to me, but everyone is listening.

"You never talk about it, but I'm not stupid, Jace. I know why you only did the obligatory social stuff with the team and stayed out of the partying scene with them."

Wes speaks up then. "We'll make our own partying scene when you're on the Stallions. The wives can even come," he teases.

Jace looks over my shoulder to Wes. "You mean we'll sit around playing chess and doing kiddie puzzles?"

"And," Zoe adds with a yawn, "we'll all go to bed at nine PM."

She leans over to kiss her husband on the forehead before adding, "Kidding, you guys chill but it's my bedtime."

Once Zoe leaves, the rest of us call it a night too. After all, we aren't the ragers we used to be. Okay, I was never a rager. But I did pretend on occasion. I give Wes strict instructions not to move the puzzle we've started and he shrugs, saying if I'd do the kiddie puzzles I'd be able to finish in one sitting.

Frankie and Lizzie stay in Jace's old room at his dad's place and we take the guest room at Gran's, which contains my old bedding and furniture. So, I guess it's really my room, but everyone's been calling it the guest room for some reason.

When we're alone in bed, Jace pulls me onto his lap for at least the third time today.

"You love me in your lap," I say softly on a giggle as I let him settle me around his hips. This time, he's in nothing but boxer briefs and I'm in sleep shorts and a thin tee shirt. I know exactly where it's leading and I lean forward to feel his lips on mine.

But instead of devouring me like I'm asking him to, Jace presses a gentle finger to my lips. "I'm sorry I've let Drake take me away from you so much. I didn't think I had a choice."

I blink at the unexpected change of direction. "You don't have to say that, Jace. You haven't done anything wrong. Until your contract with him is up, you really *don't* have a choice."

He shakes his head. "No. The contract might not end for a couple months but I'm not putting up with the bullshit until then. I know we're good. I know you trust me. But not partying and fucking around like those other guys doesn't mean I'm doing enough to earn that trust. You trust me to do what's right for us too, and I can do better. I will."

"But what about me?" I say on a whisper, my throat suddenly too dry. "Can't I do more?"

He frowns. "What do you mean?"

"I could travel with you to all these events. I could travel less for races."

His frown deepens. "No." That's it. That's all he says.

Now I'm the one frowning. "Marriages mean compromises, Jace. We each give up a little bit for each other."

"But I'm not giving up anything that matters to me here. I don't have to jump at every sponsors' beck and call. Drake makes me think I do but he's wrong, and deep down I know I have more power in the trade negotiations than he's making out. I need to take control of my career instead of letting Drake run it."

"So you're not just doing it because I miss you?" I clarify.

He runs his nose down the length of mine. "Maybe that's making me face the music and not play along, but no. I'm not a rookie anymore, it's time to step into those shoes Frankie was talking about. Be a leader. And I can't do that if I'm letting agents and sponsors dictate my life."

Melting into him, the words fall easily from my lips, "I love you, Jace Wilder."

"Love you too, Pepper Wilder." And then, finally, his lips meet mine.

Chapter Ten

PEPPER

I only get two recovery days with easy running and minimal strength training before another hard workout. For now, Lexi and Sienna are coordinating their training as much as possible with mine so that we can do some of these hard efforts together. Our training isn't perfectly aligned but we can almost always run together for long runs and easy runs. It's rare to get to do the same workout together, but they had a half marathon pace run on the agenda for this week anyway. The main difference is that my half marathon goal pace is a little faster than theirs. Still, it's worth it to me to have others to run with, so instead I add on two miles beforehand at pace so that I'm starting with them already a little fatigued.

While I know most of the best running routes around Brockton, in college we trained on trails for cross country and did workouts on the track for most of track season. Now, most of our workouts need to be on roads. Fortunately, Lexi and Sienna know of the best places with minimal traffic where we can do a nine-mile pace run.

To qualify for the Olympic marathon trials in the half marathon, I'll need to run a 5:30 mile pace. I hold this pace for the first two miles on my own before Lexi and Sienna join me and we take it back a notch. We're over a mile high at altitude, so I'm not concerned that we're pacing slightly slower than my goal pace on race day. The effort is smooth and comfortable. While I know I should be hurting more, it's a confidence boost to know that I can run this fast and still feel good at the end.

Ray doesn't see it that way. When I report to him later that day about my splits for the run, he's less than pleased with the changes I made.

"These pace runs are crucial, Pepper. You need to know what it feels like to run that pace for a long distance. The Chicago half is in two months. I think you should come down to Flagstaff and train with the team for three or four weeks. You can get in a solid block. Your 10K was great but you need these longer workouts under your belt to get the qualifying time in the half."

"I'm not going to Arizona," I tell him. Giving pushback so easily, without any thought, I realize what Jace meant the other night. He *can* take control of his career. It's easy as a professional athlete to assume you have to do what others tell you. I don't know why, but especially early on, there's this sense that it's too good to be true, that you're lucky enough to be doing what you love as a job, and you should have to do what the people in charge say in order to legitimize it. But I know I'm good enough. Especially after the 10K podium finish. After the workout today, I have total confidence in myself and I know being in Brockton training is where I need to be. I also know another race under my belt will give me that extra confidence for the Chicago half, where I hope to hit the Olympic Trials qualifying time.

"Why don't I put a half on the calendar next month? I can do it as a training run, see where I'm at," I offer.

Ray is silent for a few minutes. "That's not a bad idea. It's not what the others are doing, not my preferred approach, but I'm not opposed to it. You'll just need to keep the effort at workout level, and we'll train right through it. No resting beforehand, and no pushing to your limit at the end. I have a couple races in mind that could work."

I'm smiling at my victory when I get off the phone with Ray. I don't like having to push for what I want, what I need, for this career to work, but I'm willing to do it.

Jace is already in the weight room at Zoe and Wes's place when I arrive. They're on a ski trip, but left us free rein of their house. It's still not quite pool weather but we're taking full advantage of their gym.

I've got an hour of strength exercises to do and it's excruciating being in there with Jace as he goes through his routine nearby. Music fills the air and no words are exchanged, but the tension crackling between us is nearly unbearable. I'm in my sports bra and Jace is shirt-less, and though we didn't exactly intend for this to be some kind of buildup, I'm pulsing with need by the time I'm on my last set of lunges. Jace is hovering close by. We haven't even said anything to each other and I know by the heat in his gaze he's as wound up as I am.

"You almost finished?" he asks, voice raspy.

I lower to one more lunge and then stand. "Done."

"Thank fuck," Jace growls, coming toward me and taking my mouth in his. We're all sweaty limbs and desperation as we slip off our bottoms and tangle on the floor mat. It's fast and hard and exactly what we need as I watch him behind me in the mirror spanning the walls on both sides. I can see his front and his back with mirrors on both walls and the image is so erotic, we finish together in minutes.

"I don't think we should get a home gym," I mumble when we collapse together in a heap.

"I was thinking the exact opposite," Jace says with a devious grin.

"We need supervision. We'd never get our workouts in. I barely made it through that session and we already had sex this morning."

We do have to make up for lost time when we're together, but it never seems to be enough.

"And we've got our own hotel room tonight, so." Jace waggles his eyebrows and I giggle.

"You're insatiable," I pretend to complain.

"When it comes to you, yes, I absolutely am."

Jace gets free hotel rooms, so even though we could stay with Frankie or drive back up to Brockton after the party tonight, it's fun to take advantage of these perks. As I think that, I wonder, "Do you ever worry we'll get caught up in the money and lifestyle like Lizzie was talking about? I figured we fell in the normal category of people she described. Or trying to be despite the fame and power and privilege and whatever of the NFL."

Jace strokes a few strays from my forehead that have fallen out of my ponytail. "It's hard to think of you or us as normal, if that's what you want. We're just us, Pep. Not anything else. We have to make our own way. Fight for what works for us."

I nod. "It is a fight, isn't it? If you ride along without fighting, you can go down the wrong path. Like with Drake for you, or today when Ray tried to tell me to come out to Phoenix to train."

"You're not going?"

"Nope. I understand that the runners there are faster and there are advantages to running with them from an objective standpoint. But I'm better here. Better runner, better everything. I'm just..." I drift off, trying to think of the right words. "Where I'm supposed to be. Who I'm supposed to be, when I'm in Brockton."

Jace's expression somehow softens and darkens at the same time. Like he loves what I'm saying but it brings a cloud. I realize what I've done and try to backtrack.

"But I'm also where I'm supposed to be when I'm with you, Jace. I know that New York wants you and I know that it's far from a sure thing with Denver right now. I'll go wherever you go, okay?"

Jace nods, jaw clenching. "I know."

We're running a little late to the party at Leah and Calvin's place by the time we shower, eat and make our way down to Denver. I wasn't sure if they'd be doing dinner, and after a hard day of training I need to make sure I get something healthy in me.

The Snyders live in the trendy LoHi neighborhood downtown. They could walk to the Stallions' stadium from this location.

"Would you want to live somewhere like this if you trade to the Stallions?" I ask Jace as we wait for the elevator up to their loft. I've been hesitant to broach the topic, but curiosity gets the best of me.

Jace looks surprised and a little confused by my question. "No. We'd live in Brockton."

My heart leaps at the idea even as I register my own confusion. "But Jace, that commute would be at least an hour each way for you. I'd want to spend every night with you when we could. Not have you crashing with your friends or staying at a separate place most nights just so I could be in Brockton."

The elevator dings and we step on, Jace crowding his body around me as soon as the doors close. "Pepper, of course I'll spend every night with you when we're not traveling. Lots of people commute an hour each way. Brockton's home. I'm not doing everything I can to trade to the Stallions only to live in another town."

My hand reaches up to cup his face, finger running along his cheekbone. Jace's eyes close briefly with my touch. Sometimes we get so caught up in the logistics of our lives, I forget just how deeply this guy loves me. He doesn't think twice about making a horrible commute if it means we'll be back where we belong, where *I* belong. "I love the way you love me," I murmur.

He leans forward to kiss me as the elevator doors open, but he doesn't stop. My words must spark something in him because Jace takes what starts as a brush of our lips and devours me, caging me in with his body and letting me feel how much he wants me. Fire shoots straight to my belly with the firmness pulsing at my core, and I'm breathing hard when the dinging of the elevator doors makes Jace pull back. We're back at the bottom floor, with Angel and Tanner Walker smirking at us in amusement.

"Okay for us to join or do you two need a moment?" Tanner asks with a chuckle.

Jace doesn't move his body off of mine against the wall of the elevator, probably to hide his erection, when he responds, "Hop on, man. Good to see you." The two exchange nods, and Jace and I greet Angel as well, all of us suppressing laughter at the situation.

Jace peels himself off me, giving my hand a squeeze as the elevator goes back up, and I bite my lip with a mixture of embarrassment and lust as I watch him attempt to discreetly adjust himself.

Frankie and Lizzie are already there when we arrive. Even though I'm meeting Leah's husband Carter for the first time, I feel immediately at ease in their trendy loft. While I've never had former supermodels as girlfriends before, it already feels like I've known Angel and Leah a while, even though we've only met once before. It's funny how some people just click and it doesn't make sense. I thought I'd love running with the other pro distance runners on Newbound, and instead I felt like an outsider. Who would have thought that hanging out with three-hundred-pound football players and three women who tell me they hate running is more comfortable to me? Maybe I can relate to these women because we share the confusing identity of being in a relationship with a superstar. Who knows?

Jace is at ease too. This isn't some kind of interview for acceptance like at Frankie's foundation event, these are just people who want to make new friends, share a meal and some laughs. I didn't think I'd find a new group of friends like this after high school and college. Whether it was because we knew we wouldn't be staying or because we didn't stick around in the off-season, we didn't make friends like this in Ohio. Somehow, I never imagined we'd create new groups of friends. I just assumed our people would always be the Brockton crew. It was our own sets of friends who had merged over time, but aside from Wes, everyone in Brockton originally belonged to one of us individually. It felt right that we were making new friends together, forging our own social group with no past or history in the way. Sure, Frankie was Jace's college roommate but even with that connection to our past, this felt like the beginning of a new chapter.

"You okay?" Jace asks quietly for only me to hear. I'm sitting on a bar stool and we're all gathered around the kitchen counter. An assortment of tapas is spread out, and it looks delicious, but I'm not hungry.

I look up at Jace, who stands beside me. "Great. Why?"

He shakes his head with a little smile. "I know we had dinner before coming here but usually after a hard workout like today you could keep eating. And with all these cheeses, I'm surprised you're not digging in."

I chuckle. Yeah, he knows me well. It does seem a shame not to try some of the cheese at least, so I pick a slice off Jace's plate. After a few bites, my stomach churns, and I wash down the taste with water. I know it should taste good, but it leaves a sour aftertaste. Sometimes after a really hard workout my stomach is sensitive and I have a hard time digesting food I normally love. I'm hopeful that my body will adjust to the longer and more demanding runs once I move up to the marathon. I can't be having trouble refueling like this when my training runs are twice as long.

But I shrug it off. The transition to the road and longer distances has been going so smoothly, no need to worry about things that won't be an issue until months from now.

I'm surprised to find a voicemail from Ray when we get to the hotel later that night.

"What's he calling you about on a Saturday night? Didn't you talk to him earlier today?"

I frown as I listen to the message and tell Jace, "I told him earlier I'd do a half marathon for training in a few weeks but he found one he wants me to do this weekend in Atlanta."

It seems a little early in the training cycle to be putting in such a hard effort, especially after the eleven-mile pace run I did today, but I'm not going to question Ray's suggestion. If there's one thing I defer to him on, it's his intuition on training. If he thinks I'm in a position to keep pushing, I'm game. I've been feeling awesome.

Jace's face lights up. "I can come watch you race." He can't hide his excitement and I grin back at him.

"I'm not even supposed to race it. It's more like a training run. He thinks it will be good to do it in some humidity and heat too." Hot weather is my kryptonite, but that's why I need to suck it up and run through it. Especially with my goal race this cycle a June race in Chicago. Yuck.

Jace starts to help me undress. Not that I need it, but my limbs suddenly feel very heavy. Whether from thinking about running thirteen miles hard next weekend in gross temps or from my long day, I sag into him as he pulls my shirt over my head. Pushing me gently onto the bed to tug off my jeans, he takes a look at me. "You look wiped, Pep."

"Yeah," I agree, sleepiness taking over as I sink into the mattress.

Jace massages my muscles for a few minutes before sliding on my undies and sleep shirt. I'm already half asleep by the time he snuggles in next to me.

"Sorry I'm not a sex machine tonight, baby," I mumble as I nuzzle my face into his chest.

His chest rumbles with light laughter. "We've got our whole lives for that."

"This was one of the best days," I tell him.

He kisses me on my head but I don't even hear him respond before I'm out.

Chapter Eleven

PEPPER

I'm already more excited for the non-race in Atlanta than I was for the 10K two weeks ago simply because Jace is with me. Up to this point, most of my bigger races have been in the fall during football season and he couldn't come. I raced on the track last year for my first spring and summer as a pro, and Jace was able to come to some of those meets. Still, I've never been as into track. Now that I'm racing on the road, I think I've found the kind of racing I love best. We didn't race on roads in high school or college. Maybe it's the newness of it, or the longer distances, but I love the challenge of pacing correctly, racing in a pack like in track but not going around in a circle over and over again. The terrain isn't as fun as trails, but that means strategy comes into play more and it's still less predictable and monotonous than the track.

There are a handful of Americans in this race who are aiming for the Olympic Trials qualifying time, and a few foreigners who are here for a fast race, and, of course, a chance at the prize money. It will give me great experience for the Chicago half to run 13.1 miles with some of the world's best at this distance.

Jace gives me a kiss and a butt squeeze before hopping on a bike he rented in order to follow the race. It's seven AM and the Georgia heat is already heavy in the air when we toe the line. My plan is to grab water along the way to toss on my head and neck to cool down, but not to attempt drinking any. It takes practice to consume liquids or calories while running a 5:30 mile pace, and I don't need to start doing that until I'm preparing for the full marathon. Even in heat, I can get away with running a little over an hour without fluids.

"Runners, on your mark," the starter bellows and we take our position. Boom! The gunshot rings out and adrenaline shoots through my system on instinct. Years of race starts and the thrill hasn't diminished a bit.

The men start fifteen minutes behind us and shouldn't catch up, so it's women leading the race. A few of the top runners I recognize go out hard, faster than I'm willing to push at this stage of training. After the first frenzied half mile or so, it looks like four women are in a lead pack setting the pace. I know my pace well enough to recognize they are running closer to 5:15, and there's no way I can maintain that. Maybe it's part of their strategy but that's not mine. Not today. I settle in with the chase pack of about ten women who are running roughly 5:30 pace. Ray suggested that I don't look at my watch and go on feel, to really try to get a sense for how Olympic Trials qualifying pace feels.

I've been a little off all week. I still feel strong and smooth, but the airy runner's high vibe I've had going for weeks is finally absent. I knew it wasn't sustainable and now that I'm right in the thick of it with hard training, my body is going to start hurting.

I see Jace on the side of the road between miles three and four. He smiles at me, mouths "I love you" and gives me a double thumbs-up. Since I'm not racing and this is more of a training run, he refrains from cheering. Now, if Gran were here, she wouldn't be able to help herself. I smile inwardly at the thought, wishing I could convince her to travel to watch some of my races. I almost never compete in Colorado anymore. She did a road trip in an RV with Wallace two summers ago, but after that decided she was done traveling.

By the time we reach the halfway point, my skin is hot from the sun beating down on it. I grab a cup of water from one of the volunteers holding them out at the aid station and toss it onto my head and the back of my neck. It cools me off for about a second but I can taste the salty sweat from my forehead dripping into my mouth. While I'm uncomfortable from the heavy air, my legs still feel fresh, like we've barely started.

I'm relieved at this. I want to prove to Ray I don't need to train with the others. I want to prove to myself I can do it my way. After the halfway mark, women from our group drop like flies, and we're down to three by the time we hit mile ten. There's only three miles left and my body is still hammering out 5:30 mile pace like it's no big deal. I'm slightly amazed that I'm not sucking wind or cramping up. Even though Ray didn't want this to be a race effort, physically or mentally, I expected it would be one of the most brutal efforts of my life. Race mindset or not, this is still the longest run I've done that wasn't at easy jogging pace. Not to mention I've been logging hundred-mile weeks for over a month straight.

When our group gains on the four women in the lead pack, I start to worry. This shouldn't feel so great. Am I peaking too early? Then again, if I hit the qualifying time today, does it even matter whether I peak at the end of the training cycle? While I'm not looking at my watch, splits have been called out often enough that I have a sense we're still on 5:30 pace, and it's only been picking up as we taste the finish line. It's impossible to suppress my race instinct. I feel too strong to hold back, and I know that this feeling doesn't always come along when it needs to. So as one of the runners in our chase pack surges forward to close the gap with the lead group, I follow her.

Ray might disapprove, but it feels right in my bones. My legs want this. My eyes sting with the sweat dripping into them, and my throat is dry with thirst, but as we turn onto the main street, the finish line comes into view. I know that it's nearly another mile, which gives us time to catch the lead pack, but that's also a very long time to hold this pace. The runner beside me doesn't back down though. With the roar from the spectators growing with each step forward, she throws down the hammer.

Now would be a good time to remember I'm not supposed to be racing. But even as the burn hits my lungs and my vision blurs slightly with fatigue, my legs refuse to back down from the challenge. The lead pack is breaking apart as everyone drops the pace. When we overtake one, and then two women from the lead pack, my leg turnover picks up instinctually in an attempt to reach the next one. I don't know if I'd be doing this if not for the runner ahead of me. She's tiny, with a long braid swishing down her back, but damn she's got a motor on her.

There's less than a quarter of a mile left when we pass the third runner from the lead pack. Only one more ahead, and the runner I've been following bursts forward with so much speed I'm surprised sparks aren't shooting off the ground. I've got a decent kick, but nothing crazy, and there's no way I can stay with her. I'm holding strong at what I can only imagine is close to a five-minute pace, and my legs simply aren't capable of going faster. I watch her shoot past the lead runner and go on to break the finishing tape.

It reminds me to look at the clock above and while I knew I was running well, I'm astonished to see a 1:11 ticking above the finish line. That's well below the qualifying time for the Olympic Trials marathon. I cross the line baffled by what just happened. I'm spent, exhausted in the best way possible, and thrilled to reach my goal for this training block despite not even meaning to do it today.

My legs shake as soon as I stop running and I'm tempted to give in and collapse right there, but manage to stay upright. I congratulate the runners around me, my eyes seeking out Jace. I find him on the other side of the gate and stumble forward for a hug. The smile taking over his face hits me right in the chest, but as the adrenaline seeps out of my system, utter depletion takes over. I know this is the longest race I've ever done, but no one warned me just how rough I'd feel afterward. I'm parched, and I know the hot sun beating on me isn't helping matters. An official hands me a bottle of water after Jace releases me and I start to screw off the top with shaky hands. Darkness creeps into my vision, and I stumble backward, needing support. I feel Jace reach over the barrier to hold my back just as I get the top off the water. But the bottle suddenly feels too heavy to bring up to my mouth, and blackness takes over.

JACE

I watched the bottle of water slip from her fingers and realized what was happening. My hand supported her back but I couldn't keep her from falling with the barrier between us. She went down like a sack of potatoes. Just, *whoosh*, on the ground. I managed to lean over to keep her head from crashing and then jumped over the barrier to her side. Her eyes fluttered open again as I propped her up in my lap.

Pepper's face had been red from heat and exertion a moment ago and was now ashen. "I fainted," she slurred, confusion clouding her face.

My heart was racing with fear and worry, but the medics who swarmed in acted like this was part and parcel of finishing a half marathon. I rubbed my hands over her arms and legs, wanting to soothe the goosebumps popping up and warm the skin that was turning clammy. Her legs, now more toned than ever from the mileage and weights she'd been hammering out, were shaking slightly, and my blood whooshed in my ears as I tried to stay focused on what the medics were doing and saying. They took her pulse.

"She fainted once before," I informed them, realizing that I was the best one to answer some of the questions while Pepper remained less than fully coherent. "It was years ago, in high school, and it was in the middle of a race. I don't know if this was the same though." With the crowds all around, and some other pros and elites still in the finish area, I didn't want to elaborate. Back then, she'd fainted more from the mental pressure she'd put on herself than from a physical reaction.

"It looks like heat exhaustion and dehydration," one of the medics said. "Let's get her in the tent to examine her better and get some fluids in her."

The other medic nodded at Pepper. "Congratulations, ma'am," he said in a southern drawl, and I didn't like the way he smiled at her.

Pepper's lower lip trembled slightly when she thanked him, and I wondered if she was about to cry from happiness at how well she did, or because she was freaked out by what just happened.

There was an awkward moment when the medics asked me to move so they could carry her to the medical tent and I refused. She hadn't broken any bones and didn't need to be held in any particular position. This was a job for her husband. I scooped her up off the ground, her body feeling too light for a woman so damn strong. With nothing on her but booty running shorts and a racing top that was hardly more than a sports bra, I wasn't too thrilled about laying her out on a bed in the medical tent for a couple of young dudes to poke around at. Fortunately, a slightly older woman took over from there, asking Pepper questions about how she felt, putting a blanket over her, and encouraging her to sip water.

"Don't worry, sweetie," the woman said, "I work at elite endurance events all the time and lots of the pros go into a little shock after a hard effort like that. Doesn't help that it's hot in Georgia."

I could tell that Pepper was soothed by the woman's sympathy and the knowledge that this wasn't an unusual occurrence. The racing in my heart slowed slightly as a little color returned to Pepper's cheeks. I was holding Pepper's hand, rubbing my thumb over hers, when her coach, Ray, burst through the tent entrance.

He nodded at me in greeting before pulling up a chair next to Pepper. "What happened out there?" The guy was a former Olympic marathon runner and was well respected by everyone at these races. He was at the start beside Pepper but stayed behind to talk to a couple of his male runners who started after her.

Pepper stiffened a little, and I narrowed my eyes at her reaction. It was like she was gathering her courage, preparing to defend herself. "I know it doesn't seem like it," she said, gesturing to the blanket over her body and the tent generally, "but I actually felt really strong out there. I didn't mean to go so hard. I didn't even realize I was pushing my body so hard that this would happen. Honestly, Ray, I felt smooth and solid just like we planned until the last mile or so."

Ray's expression was unreadable. "I know. I was able to catch you on the course between miles eight and ten. You looked great. And based on your finishing time you didn't blow up. But I'm really concerned about your body's reaction to all of it. For such a great run, it doesn't quite add up to me."

Pepper's voice was small when she asked, "Does this mean I'm not cut out for the marathon? If I go into shock from a race that felt great that's only half the distance, that's not a good sign for my future as a marathon runner." I was surprised by the emotion shaking in her voice. I knew that she wanted to make the Olympic team in the marathon, but I didn't realize until this moment how devastated she'd be if it wasn't in the cards. It's not like they have a half marathon at the Olympics and the next longest Olympic event is the 10K, a track event, which is far from her favorite type of race.

Ray smiled. "Calm down. Don't get dramatic on me," he said. "You've now got ten months to prepare for the Olympic Trials in the marathon. That's plenty of time to shock your body a few more times so it won't be traumatized when the time comes." He was smiling, even joking a little, but the idea didn't sit well with me. It couldn't be sustainable to keep pushing her body to this point, could it?

Chapter Twelve

PEPPER

I expected to be more embarrassed about ending up in the medical tent, but the excitement over hitting such a fast time overshadows anything else. Mostly. Back in Brockton two days later, I'm still a little confused about why it happened and how to fix it. Last time I had a weird fainting spell while running it was because I put too much pressure on myself. I didn't feel that way at all for this race, didn't even treat it like a race. The other time was because someone drugged me, which couldn't have happened in this case because there's no way I would've run so well.

Ray and Jace both suggest getting blood tests and a general health check-up to make sure I don't have any deficiencies. I did miss my period a couple of weeks ago, but that's happened before when I increase my mileage. It's pretty common, and while I know it's not healthy to continue missing periods, I'm pretty sure I'm fueling properly and figure there's not much else I could do. Maybe it would help to see a nutritionist, start drinking weird protein shakes like Jace.

I'm at the primary care office in Brockton, waiting for the doctor to come in for a brief chat. I've peed in a cup and had my blood drawn, which almost made me pass out again with how much they took, but I won't get my results from the blood test for a few more days. At the urging of the medics I took the day after the race completely off from training, my first full day off in years without even cross training. It was seriously weird to sit around all day with Jace and snuggle, watching movies and doing puzzles. I definitely soaked it in but now I'm restless as hell and can't wait to get out of here to go on a run with Lexi and Sienna. My legs feel airy and itchy, like they might shoot out and kick someone at any moment. They're not used to rest and the lack of weighty fatigue is unnerving.

If one day of rest does this, imagine how well I'll race at the Chicago half after resting for a week or two! I can't decide if I just had a professional breakthrough at my last two races or if the real one is just around the corner.

"Mrs. Wilder." Dr. Burch greets me with a friendly smile and a handshake before pulling up her rolling stool and sitting down on it. She's been my doctor for almost two years now, since I graduated from CU.

Her smile wavers for a minute and I'm a little confused as to why she would look nervous. "Congratulations. You're pregnant."

I stay frozen, sitting on my hands, but my swinging legs stop. Blood rushes in my head and I blink several times. "What did you say?"

"Your urine sample confirmed that you're pregnant, Mrs. Wilder. I'm guessing by the notes here that this isn't what you were expecting?" Her eyes dart to the little mini computer thingy in her lap.

"Um. I think you must be mistaken. That's not possible. I'm on the pill. I don't even get my period consistently. I just qualified for the Olympic Trials two days ago in the half marathon. There's just no way." It would be really easy for them to get the wrong pee sample, actually. We put the cup in a little box after peeing. I bet they accidentally switched mine with the lady who was called in right before me from the waiting room.

"Well, the chances of becoming pregnant on the pill are less than one percent but it's not impossible. And it's possible even without regular periods. How long have they been irregular?"

Blood rushes in my head again and my chest squeezes. This can't be right. "I missed my last one. Before that they'd been regular for almost a year. But I've lost it before when I increase my mileage. I really can't be pregnant. Can you do an ultrasound or something to check?" I cringe at the desperation in my voice and the pity in her smile.

"I was going to suggest just that. We can see how far along you are."

I squeeze my eyes shut at her refusal to acknowledge the possibility that this is a mistake, but follow her orders to lie back. My heart rate picks up for an entirely different reason when she starts gooping gel onto what looks like a giant dildo instead of onto my stomach.

"Early on we use a transvaginal ultrasound. It will be slightly uncomfortable at first but no worse than a pap smear."

She arranges my feet on the awful little metal things that look like torture devices before easing the most awkward medical tool ever inside of me. I mean really, in this day and age you'd think they'd have something better. I'm distracting myself from what's about to happen, what's really going on, by trying to stir up some outrage toward the medical device companies that must be run by men, when I hear a steady thudding noise. It's faint over the whooshing sound on the little ultrasound screen, but it's unmistakable.

I glance over at it, unable to tell what the fuzzy black and white lines mean, when Dr. Burch points to a tiny mark. "It's no mistake, Pepper," she says with conviction. "That's the baby's heartbeat we're listening to. And that's the baby."

The baby. *Baby?*

My mind reels as it struggles through layers of disbelief. But the heartbeat is still pounding on the machine, and the little blob on the screen is bobbing to the beat. There is no mistake. This is real.

I'm having a baby.

———

Two days ago my body went into some kind of physical shock, now I'm in a mental shock. I can't remember anything else the doctor told me after the ultrasound except for the due date. November twentieth. Three months before the Olympic marathon trials.

I should be going straight to Jace, who's working out with Wes at his place, but without even realizing it, I've driven to the water hole we used to swim at. My limbs are on autopilot as I park Gran's old car and get out, walking down the little path leading to the river. We used to jump off the rocks into the freezing water and then warm up on the rocks. No one else is around late morning on a cool spring day and I lean against a tree, taking deep breaths. I need to be alone to process this. What it means.

I'm still grappling with the reality that we're in the less than point three percent who get pregnant on birth control. I thought they only said that to avoid lawsuits. I didn't know it could actually happen. Especially when I take the pills regularly. *Especially* when I'm training so hard and already putting my body through so much. I can't believe I ran like I did the other day. How was that possible? My mind keeps wanting to reach the conclusion that it's *not* possible, that it isn't real. I imagined everything. But as I stand here alone with only the sounds of the rustling leaves, I already know it's real. Because I don't feel totally alone.

I shake my head at the thought and find my hands are resting on my stomach. There's a little human hanging out with me. A little Wilder baby.

"Come on," I whisper. "Let's go tell your dad about you."

An unexpected wave of nerves hits as I drive to Wes's house. First denial, then shock, confusion, followed by acceptance, and now I'm nervous to tell my husband? Maybe there's some truth about the whole hormonal emotions thing because I can barely keep up with myself.

How will Jace react? What if he's angry? I shouldn't have been running so intensely. It could have hurt the baby. Less than an hour after discovering I'm going to be a mom and my mindset has already shifted so drastically.

I park in Wes and Zoe's driveway and as I get out of the car, a smile takes over my face. And cue the next emotional onslaught. Joy. Excitement. I start to jog into the house but stop myself. I should've asked the doctor about that. I see pregnant women running all the time but after what happened on Sunday, maybe I shouldn't.

Instead, I skip inside and downstairs to the gym, where the guys are lifting weights and loud music is practically shaking the house down. Jace spots me in the mirror and raises his eyebrows in question before getting off the bench to walk toward me. He knows I was meant to run after the appointment, and I can see concern in his gaze when he reaches me. I gesture to the hallway where we can be alone and he follows me back up the stairs.

When I sit down on the couch beside him and take his hands in mine, color drains from his face. "Pep, what is it?"

"I'm pregnant."

The expression on his face must mirror the one I had when I learned the news because he just continues to stare at me like he didn't hear me correctly.

"You're..." He searches my face before his eyes drop to my flat stomach and scan my body. "We're having a baby?" he whispers in reverence.

I don't know what I expected but it wasn't Jace Wilder's eyes filling with tears. My husband doesn't cry. He shows emotion to me now, but he doesn't spontaneously break into tears.

He blinks them away, still whispering when he leans down and presses the palm of his hand to my belly. "Holy shit, Pep."

He grins up at me. "Did I really do that? Even with you on birth control?"

I giggle. "*We* did it. Of course you would assume it was all you."

"Tell me everything. How'd they find out? How far along are you? What did the doctor say about you fainting on Sunday? Did that hurt the baby?" Jace leans down and lifts my shirt up like he can see the baby through my belly button. "Are you going to be okay?" I can't tell if that last question is directed at me or the baby.

"Everything's good. I think. Honestly I barely heard anything she said once I saw the baby on the ultrasound."

"You did an ultrasound already?" Jace's eyes widen. "Wait. Can we go back and do another one? Shit. I should have gone with you today."

"Jace, it's fine. We don't make a habit of going to each other's doctor's appointments together. That would be weird. We thought I was low on iron, not pregnant."

If Jace was protective before, I'm going to have to prepare for it to go up about a hundred levels. At the moment, it's adorable, but I can see already the lack of control over the situation will be a struggle for him.

I tell him everything I know, which mostly consists of the due date and the fact that the baby has a beating heart. And also that Dr. Burch didn't seem too concerned about the stress I put the baby under on Sunday, given everything looked good and normal. Obviously, I'll have to make another appointment soon to talk about what kind of exercise I can do. And I need to call my agent, and Ray. First I have to tell Gran, and Zoe and Wes, and Jim, and...

I let out a deep breath and Jace pulls me close. He brushes his lips against mine. "I know this is a little weird, but I want you so bad right now it's painful."

At his words, heat flares low in my belly. My hand drifts between us to confirm what he's said and Jace lets out a harsh breath. "I seriously want to go back to the doctor right now," he confesses, his voice strained, "to check about everything we can and can't do. Part of me wants to carry you everywhere to keep you safe but my dick just wants to show off. It's so fucking proud of itself."

I burst into laughter and Jace smirks at me with one eyebrow raised. "Less than point three percent, huh?"

"What's less than point three percent?" Wes asks, wiping a towel over his forehead as he comes up the basement stairs.

Jace and I glance at each other. Do we tell him now? We still haven't told Gran or Jim. And aren't you supposed to wait until the second trimester or something? I thought I'd heard that. But I can't lie to Wes.

Jace makes the decision for me when he announces, "We're having a baby." There's so much pride in his voice, and I let him have the ego boost for the moment. Not that he needs it.

Wes's eyes widen and he starts to smile before frowning. "Are you fucking with me right now?" he asks, doubt filling the question.

"Nope. November twentieth due date," I confirm, noting the pride in my own voice. Man, we're pathetic. It's not like we did anything special other couples don't do, but I've never been prouder of anything else. It's kind of a ridiculous phenomenon actually.

"But you just qualified for the Olympic Trials in the half marathon two days ago," Wes states, still in denial mode. I can relate.

I just shrug, a grin plastered to my face.

When it sinks in that we're not messing with him, Wes's smile takes over. "I'm gonna be an uncle."

He tries to tackle us in hugs but he's dripping sweat so I let him pat my head instead.

Seems our little family is growing.

Chapter Thirteen

PEPPER

I'm riding a new kind of high as I revel in Jace's total awestruck reaction, our shared joy in creating this life together. We're intoxicated with amazement and wonder, unable to stop sharing looks, touches, smiles, kisses. It lasts through sharing the news with Gran, then Jim, and slowly our friends. I'd blown off Lexi and Sienna earlier for a run and even though the news is still fresh, it's impossible to keep it to myself. The excitement is practically bursting out of me and no negative emotions can pop this bubble. Worry, doubt, disappointment at how this will change everything for my running career, it's all irrelevant to me in this moment.

The realities don't hit me until Ray calls the next morning. I don't want to answer. I'm not ready to tell him. I'm not ready to handle his reaction, the reaction of my sponsors, or discuss it with my agent Finn. All those details seem so cumbersome and irrelevant right now.

Gran and Jace hover over me while I eat my breakfast. Neither comments when I ignore Ray's call.

"Did Dr. Burch say anything about morning sickness?" Jace asks, scooting his chair closer to me and pushing a glass of juice in my direction. "Isn't it normal to be sick in the mornings at seven weeks along?"

I put down the toast I was about to bite into. "I didn't think to ask that. Let's call over there. We should make another appointment. I have a million questions now that I'm not in shock."

"She ain't gonna be able to tell ya much, kids. Nothing and every-thing about bein' pregnant is normal," Gran says from her seat on the other side of the table, two hands grasping her coffee mug.

Jace and I stare at her and she chuckles at our confusion. "If you were sick every morning, you'd be worryin' you weren't normal. You're not sick and now you're still frettin'. Just relax." She waves a hand before taking a sip of coffee. "Obviously you're supposed to have this baby if it came so easy. What should we name him?"

"Him?" Jace straightens beside me, ears perked up.

Gran shrugs. "I don't want to call the baby an 'it' and I'm bettin' on a boy if I have to pick."

"Let's give it – I mean, the baby – a gender-neutral name while I'm pregnant."

"Let's call him Baby Wilder," Jace suggests.

"Or her," I remind them both.

Jace mutters. "A girl? A baby girl? Shit."

I study Jace, trying to picture a girl version of him.

Another ringing phone slices through the air. Can't we get a moment of peace around here? This time, it's Frankie calling for Jace. Of course, Jace has been beaming with more pride than I've ever seen emanating from him since I shared the news.

Jace stands up to take the call and immediately informs Frankie he's going to be a dad.

No winning game from any sport, not even our own wedding, have I ever seen him look so damn full of life. Like he rules the world. Man, he's come so far. I can't imagine the old Jace reacting like this, embracing this role like he owns it. Like he'd been born to be a dad. To father *my* children.

Gran's grinning one of her loony toothy smiles when she sees the dreamy look in my eyes. Yeah, they're filled with tears. "Now that, that's definitely normal pregnancy hormones. Prepare yourself for an emotional rollercoaster, baby girl."

I'm still trying to finish eating breakfast when my phone rings again. This time it's Finn, my agent. He congratulated me by text after the race and emailed me to let me know he'd be calling about some new sponsorship opportunities arising from the podium finish and qualifying time.

I can't ignore Finn's call like I can Ray's, and that tells me a lot right there. Of course, Finn knows about me fainting after the race on Sunday, and his first question is how I'm feeling.

"I feel great," I tell him truthfully.

"Still waiting to see if the blood work comes up with anything? What'd the doctor have to say?"

I hesitate only a moment before giving him the news. "I'm pregnant. Seven weeks."

Silence. I know that it might have been wiser to wait to share this, to come up with a plan. But unlike with Ray, or Jace with his agent, I trust Finn. I want to able to lean on someone in my professional circle, on my team, who can help me come up with a strategy on how to address this with my sponsors and fans, the race directors expecting me to show at their races, all that stuff.

"Congratulations, Pepper." I know I've done the right thing when that's his initial response, even if it's coated in a bit of disbelief. "I just can't believe you ran a 1:11 half seven weeks pregnant. That's really something."

"Me neither," I admit.

"This gives us a really exciting direction to go in. Pregnancy and motherhood in the running community is a hot area, and I'm sure we can get sponsors lining up to get you in their maternity running gear and trying their strollers, all that fun stuff." Finn pauses to chuckle. "Sorry, don't want to overwhelm you but my head is already spinning with the new direction we'll be headed. When I called I expected to talk about your race plans now that you've got the qualifying time under your belt. I didn't think we'd be reevaluating how we market you. But I'm happy for you, Pepper."

"Thanks Finn, that means a lot."

We spend a few more minutes speaking about how and when we'll break the news to my sponsors, and Finn mentions several elite women he can put me in touch with who had babies mid-running career. I'm so early in my own career, none of my peers have been pregnant. Few are even married. The runners on Newbound are older but none of them have kids or seem to be planning on it anytime soon. It would be great to speak with other elite runners about how they handled training, sponsors and all that stuff.

As I end my call with Finn, Jace returns from his conversation with Frankie. He walks toward me with the same confidence and authority that always radiates from him, but it's stronger, more resolute. Is it possible just the news of our growing family can give a guy like Jace Wilder a new sense of purpose? It hasn't even been twenty-four hours and the shift inside of us is unmistakable.

Dave senses it too, darting back and forth between us. We kiss Gran goodbye and take Dave on a walk, hand in hand on our favorite trail. So many memories are with us on the path that winds up the foothills.

We walk in easy silence and I try to think about whether my body feels any different. I listen to my breathing, and pay attention to my legs and stomach. Everything seems to be the same as always, except for the knowledge there's a little person inside me. I know my stomach was a little off the other night at the Snyders' place, but aside from the strange reaction after the race on Sunday, it's no wonder I didn't realize what was happening. I feel fit, strong, healthy.

When we reach one of the clearings with a view overlooking the city, Jace leads me to a boulder and hoists me to sit atop it, jumping up behind me. I rest back into him and sigh. There's a lot to figure out, now more than ever, but somehow, I'm more at peace today than I was before learning the news. It feels like it'll all fall into place and work itself out.

"You seem good, Pep. I thought this morning it might sink in what this means for the trials. The Olympics. But you aren't upset."

I lean back to look at him so he can see that his assessment is right. "I know. If you told me before that this was going to happen I would have been a wreck. But now that it actually has, everything else is less important. I'm too happy to be sad about what I'm giving up." I shake my head at the words. "No, that's the thing. It doesn't feel like I'm giving up anything really. Isn't that crazy?"

Jace's hand runs down my arm, landing on my belly. He splays his palm protectively over me. "Nope. I'm with you, Pep. If it was you and Baby Wilder or football, it wouldn't even be a question. There'd be no regret. The only question for me now is what I'll do if I don't trade to the Stallions."

I place my hand over his. "We'll figure it out."

Jace's voice is determined when he tells me, "We're not going to New York. I already didn't feel right about working that angle as a potential option and now I know it's not right for us. I thought I could do a year or two there before trading again but we need to be closer to home."

"What are the other options if not New York or Colorado?"

Jace rattles off a few other places that have shown interest, explaining the various chances of becoming first-string QB on those teams. "I think wherever I land next season, you should stay here in Brockton."

I sit up all the way at that declaration. "What? No. I need to be with you, Jace. Not here."

Jace looks at me hard, jaw set. "I'll be gone too much for games. You won't know anyone. What if something happens? Pep, you need your family. Buns, Wallace, Lulu, Zoe, Wes, Lexi," he starts to list everyone off but I get the point and cut him off.

"You, Jace. I need you."

Jace swallows hard and I see a storm behind those bright green eyes. This uncertainty, this lack of control for his future, our future, it's tearing him up. Now more than ever. Maybe only the mom gets filled with a sense of peace and ease when expecting a baby. I was just as uptight about all of it as he was, and now I feel settled, like it's going to fall into place. Here, or somewhere else, we'll be a family unit. Jace will come around. We should know in the next month where we'll be, and that will calm Jace. I hope.

Chapter Fourteen

JACE

I was helping Pep off the boulder for the walk home when my phone rang. Seeing it was Drake again, I let out a curse. I should've left the phone at home, let us have at least this one moment uninterrupted.

"Just answer it, Jace," Pepper said with a sigh. "See what he wants so he'll stop calling."

Right. Like this asshole would ever stop calling. If it wasn't one thing, it was another. He saw me as his next big paycheck. Scratch that. I already was his biggest paycheck of all his clients. But he thought he could use me to make a real name for himself. If I wasn't over it before, I was now.

I put the phone to my ear. "What?"

"Hello to you too, sunshine," Drake mocked. He thought he was funny, that we were bros. That alone told me the guy wasn't so smart.

I didn't respond, and after a beat of silence, Drake told me why he called. Another publicity opportunity in New York.

"I told you, Drake. I'm done with parading around New York. I'm not traveling there again. Especially after the shit you pulled with Madeline Brescoll and the New York Times photographer."

Drake ignored that comment. "What are you planning to do if the

Stallions deal falls through, Jace? I haven't followed up with any of the other teams because you wanted to limit your travel."

Bullshit. I've figured enough out now to understand that trading to a different team didn't require the level of travel he'd been pushing to New York. He wanted the bigger payout if I landed with the Super Bowl reigning champs. The prestige it would give him.

"You know what, Drake? I think I got it from here. I'll handle the trade negotiations until our contract is up."

Drake sputtered through the line. "Excuse me?" His voice was shrill, like a whiny kid.

"You heard me. I'll handle it from here. Have your assistant send me all the docs."

"Jace, we have a contract."

"A contract that ends in three weeks."

"Yes, and those are a crucial three weeks. If we don't complete the deal, what are you going to do, get a new agent mid-negotiations? It doesn't work that way. What's really going on here?"

Like hell I was going to share the news with this prick. He'd twist it and taint it. I knew what he was about.

"I said I'll do it alone. I know the contract doesn't allow me to take on a new agent until our term is over." I'd spoken with a lawyer about it a few weeks ago, just wanting to consider all my options. Until this moment, I'd thought I could deal with Drake for a few more weeks. Now I was going with my gut instinct. Which told me Drake would sabotage me if I didn't take the reins. Possibly even manipulate the situation to force a trade to New York.

Drake rambled something about a breach of contract, his own team of lawyers, and that I should reconsider, all in the same breath. Threatening me while also trying to get me to trust him with my career, my life? I didn't think so.

When I ended the call, I felt a hell of a lot lighter.

"You just fired Drake," Pepper said, confusion clouding the state-ment. "I thought you couldn't do that."

"Officially he's not fired. I'll still have to give him a cut of whatever deal I make with the next trade. Happy to do it to avoid a legal dispute. But I'm not letting him be involved anymore. I don't trust him. And I'm not letting him parade me around and push me to New York so he can rise the ranks."

"You ran all this by the lawyer you spoke with last month?"

I could tell Pepper wanted to be happy for me but was worried I'd acted on a whim, made a rash decision I'd regret.

I pulled her to me and walked her backward until she was leaning against a tree. "Ran it by the lawyer, Pep. I was going to ride it out and let Drake do his thing until the contract was up, but this was another option I had that I decided to take. I can cut him out of the discussions with the Stallions. I'm not going to keep discussions going with New York anyway. Frankie's already got his agent ready to go for me as soon as the contract with Drake is done."

I watched this sink in, and if possible, Pepper looked even more relaxed that she'd been before. "I knew it would all fall into place."

My lips met hers as some of her optimism seeped into me. The gentle kiss turned heated when she opened her mouth and let my tongue inside.

I knew that Drake would make this hell, but I'd keep the shitstorm from Pepper. I needed to put everything I had into making a deal with the Stallions, even if it meant less money, less prestige, less sponsorships, whatever. I didn't care about that, never really did. But Drake did, and he was not going to let it go easy.

As long as Pepper stayed in this easy mindset, where nothing could touch her, I didn't really give a shit about the rest.

Chapter Fifteen

PEPPER

We arrange a phone call with Dr. Burch, who reassures us that everything is normal with the baby and the blood tests all came back looking good too. She thinks that the physical exertion at the race, coupled with the heat and humidity, drained me more than normal because of the pregnancy. While she doesn't recommend repeating those conditions or pushing my body so hard again during pregnancy, she doesn't think there was any lasting damage.

"So, what do you recommend with running and training during pregnancy?" I ask.

"Lots of women exercise through pregnancy. Some even run marathons. I really think it's a matter of listening to your body. Just because you're a professional athlete doesn't mean your body will handle exercise well during pregnancy."

This advice really isn't all that helpful. Sure, she's given me a green light to keep running and training, and when it comes to running I like to think I've really fine-tuned the body-listening thing. But based on what happened on Sunday, I'm not so sure it translates in this context.

I point out my dilemma to her. "But I felt amazing in that race right through the finish. And then I fainted and suffered dehydration."

We have her on speakerphone and Jace sits beside me on the couch, rubbing circles on my back and trying not to interrupt.

Dr. Burch mulls this over and then says, "In your case then, where you're so used to pushing through pain that it feels normal, I would err on the side of less training. Stick with mild exercise."

I want to explain that this really isn't helpful either. At all. Mild exercise? What the hell does that mean to a professional athlete? I'm going to need to reach out to those mom runners Finn mentioned ASAP and get some real advice.

I refrain from sharing my frustration with Dr. Burch and she signs off, letting us know we'll see her next at our twelve-week appointment. It seems like we should be seeing her sooner than that, but I guess this is standard. I should be grateful everything's normal and I don't need to come in earlier.

The lack of direction about how to handle training, my *job*, while pregnant is a little disconcerting, but I'm really not all that worried about it. While Finn emailed me some women I can reach, I'm not quite ready to share the news with everyone in the running community. I still haven't told Ray. Instead, I spend hours researching the elite runners and their various approaches to training while pregnant. There's more information than I expect, and I discover that Finn was right, there's a lot of interest in this area. But while there's a lot of information to take in, it doesn't necessarily give me answers. Some pro distance runners trained up to a hundred miles a week all the way until the third trimester, while others didn't run at all and only cross-trained. I guess Dr. Burch was right about it being different for everyone.

By Friday, I can't ignore Ray any longer, and I take a deep breath before calling him.

When he answers, I'm surprised at how frantic he sounds. "Pepper. I haven't been able to reach you all week. What's going on?"

"Sorry. It's just been, um, crazy."

Ray coaches fourteen other elite runners, mostly women and a couple men, but all with similar chances as me at making the next Olympic team. It's not unusual for us to go several days or even a week or two without connecting by phone. I suppose with how things were left, what with me ending up in the medical tent, I shouldn't have left him hanging for so long.

"What did the doctor have to say?"

"Well, it wasn't an iron deficiency."

There's a silence as he waits for me to fill him in, and I'm more nervous to share the news with him than I have been for anyone else. I just don't know how he'll react.

"I'm seven weeks pregnant. Almost eight now, actually."

Of all the reactions I expected, his response is not one I could have imagined. "You aren't keeping it, are you?"

My stomach churns at the question and I experience my first wave of true nausea since becoming pregnant. "Excuse me?" Maybe I misunderstood.

"You're on fire in your running career. You've qualified for the trials and have ten months to prepare for it without worrying about any other races now that you've got the qualifying time. You're still so young, Pepper. You can't give up your chance at the Olympics. Not now."

I shake my head at everything he's saying, my eyes burning. "I'm having the baby, Ray. There will be other Olympics. Other races." My hand hurts from gripping the phone so tightly, and I wish it was Ray's neck. I've never been a violent person but I have the urge to punch something right now, and if Ray was here in front of me, I'd like it to be his face.

Ray switches tactics when he hears the emotion behind my response. He starts to talk about all the training options out there, zero gravity treadmills, water running, and gives examples of those few pros who did run high mileage throughout their pregnancies. But I don't want to have any goals or expectations for my fitness during this time. I don't want a race on the calendar right after the due date. I don't want to be tempted to do more than I can handle or rush through breast feeding so I can race a marathon faster.

While Ray gains momentum about how I could set some record for bouncing back post-baby with a debut marathon win, I come to a decision that's easier than I think.

I quit the Newbound team. The most prestigious marathon training group in the country, maybe the world, and I have zero regrets about saying goodbye. I know how Jace felt when he dropped Drake. There used to be indecisiveness and uncertainty about these big decisions but the clarity now is startling. It's obvious that I don't belong with Ray or his group of Newbound runners. While I sensed that truth earlier, my judgment was clouded somehow. I don't care if people say I'm nuts to leave him to train with my old college teammates, whose accolades are one-tenth that of the least accomplished Newbound runner. It's right for me.

I'm sitting on the bed staring into space when Jace comes in a few minutes later.

"Pep? How'd the call go with Ray?" Jace has been hovering all week, and I've let him. I'll need to kick him out and tell him he can go to the gym at some point, but I've been enjoying our cocoon.

I thought I was sitting here reveling in my decision, feeling good, but I'm hit with an onslaught of anger as I try to tell him what Ray said. My lip trembles, and as I say the words, I find myself dissolving into full body-wracking sobs. Jace holds me and hushes me as he tries to figure out what I'm telling him.

Gran was right about the emotional rollercoaster. This is one hell of a confusing ride.

"Pep, you haven't run since Sunday. That's five days. Maybe you'll feel better if you go on a little jog." Jace speaks quietly as he runs a hand over my head like I'm a little kid in need of soothing. I kind of feel like one right now.

"You think I should run?"

"Dr. Burch says it's fine. You don't need to run for hours or do hill sprints or anything."

"I'm just confused. I don't remember how to just run based on feel. I had a plan and now it's gone. I'm not sad about that but I'm not sure what to do now. And I don't have a coach anymore to tell me what to do."

"Why don't you do some shorter easier runs for a little while and when you're ready you can talk to some of the runners Finn told you about and think about how to approach it? Running is such a part of you I can't imagine you won't want to keep doing it, but you don't have to stick to any sort of plan."

I sigh into Jace's chest. "You should just be my coach," I say, mostly joking. He knows enough about running by now that he could probably wing it and do okay, but really only when it comes to the mental aspects of the sport.

I'm grateful he's encouraging me to run. I wasn't sure how he felt about it, if he would want me to stop. With Jace unable to control anything else about the pregnancy, I was willing to concede on some points for the sake of his sanity, but I wasn't sure how I'd feel if he asked me to stop running. I'm still not sure how I feel about it myself as I change into my running clothes and lace up my sneakers.

"Want me to come with?" Jace asks.

He occasionally joins me when I have a short easy run, but he doesn't like to go longer than four miles and I almost never run shorter than that these days. It will be different now, but I need a moment to clear my head. It's my first run *knowing* that I'm pregnant. Somehow, it feels like a big step.

"In the last ten minutes, I've gone from nervous to talk to Ray, sick to my stomach with his response, to resolute in my decision. Then I think I was amazed and happy by how easy and clear-headed I felt about the decision to leave Newbound, and well," I gesture to the bed, "then I was a blubbering, angry, upset mess from what Ray said and how confused I am about what this all means."

Jace nods patiently as I speak, eyeing me warily like I might burst into another fit of tears. He should be wary. "I feel completely unstable right now," I say on a long sigh. "Clear-headed and floating with ecstasy one second and a complete disaster the next. I seriously need a run."

Jace continues nodding, eyes wide. "I know, baby, that's why I suggested it. But you didn't answer my question. Do you want me to come with?"

Oh yeah. Apparently on top of all that I can't follow a conversation. I bite my lip to keep from laughing at the situation. At myself. "No. I'll bring my phone but I want to run alone." I don't need to explain to Jace. He knows me and knows not to be offended that I don't want to run with him. I need that feeling of my feet pounding on dirt, fresh mountain air, and the steady beat of my legs moving along. Given he hasn't left my side for more than five minutes since learning about the baby, I know he'll make me bring my phone anyway.

"Love you," he tells me with a kiss on my cheek. And then he crouches down and lifts my shirt to kiss the spot above the waistband of my shorts. "Love you too, Lil' Wilder."

I groan. "You're going to make me cry. Stop it."

When he smirks up at me, another rush flows through me. Want. If I'm this crazy and all over the place for the next seven months, we're in serious trouble. I need to get out of here before I lose my mind.

Chapter Sixteen

PEPPER

The next morning we wake to find our phones blowing up. Someone finally decided to run with the photos of Jace and me each with different people weeks ago, when Jace was in New York and I raced in Boston. Given who the other people are – from our hometown, attractive, and already in the spotlight themselves – we knew this might happen. That doesn't make the article any less ugly. I skim through it, the sick feeling growing with each speculation. A "source" close to the couple said that Madeline Brescoll is Jace Wilder's ex-girlfriend and they had a long history in high school. They've recently reconnected and seemed cozy. Another "source" said similar things about me and Ryan, that we have a history and I'm now running with him regularly in Brockton. It's gossip, but the news website has slightly more clout than a gossip rag, and the writing comes across as journalistic enough that some people might take it seriously.

I toss my phone to the side. "I'd ignore this and brush it off, but what's the deal with the 'source' they quoted? That's a little disturbing." Jace sits next to me in bed, scrolling through the article on his laptop.

Jace doesn't look up when he answers. "It's Drake. No one would bother publishing this story unless someone was really pushing for it. It's not news. It's not even gossip people would be interested in normally. Drake's being an asshole. Throwing a tantrum because he's not getting his way and hoping I'll react and beg for his help."

I shake my head, wondering how a dude in his thirties can be so immature. He must have been a spoiled little punk as a kid. "Let's make sure we don't raise this baby to be a little shit like Drake, 'kay?" I snuggle up to Jace, wanting to lighten the mood and brush this off as nothing more than a nuisance.

Jace closes his computer and pulls my body on top of his.

"Little Wilder is going to be perfect," he tells me, kissing me on the nose.

There's a knock on the door and Lulu calls, "Kids, breakfast is ready! It's gettin' cold!"

Jace and I smile at each other. We're both thinking the same thing. It's probably time to get our own place, but we need to figure out where we'll be long-term first. And really, it's no hurry. Who can complain about having all their meals cooked? The lack of privacy is a bit irritating at times, but I will miss all the commotion and craziness too.

Over the next couple weeks, I run almost every day with Lexi and Sienna on their shorter, easier runs, or Zoe, Wes, or some of my friends from high school. While I know I could theoretically train harder during pregnancy, backing off feels like the right thing to do. Not to mention, I don't really have a coach right now and I've got no idea what my plan is down the road. I guess I'm waiting for Jace to figure out where he'll be, which should be any day now. Draft contracts have been exchanged with the Stallions but I know Jace hasn't shared all of the complicated details, like the fallout with Drake. I guess as long as he's here with me in Brockton for the moment, I'm cool staying in the dark on the messier points.

In some ways, it's been the best couple of weeks I've had in a long time. We celebrated my twenty-fourth birthday with a low-key party at the Old House Tavern where I used to work. Neither of us is traveling and without a demanding training schedule, I'm able to hang out and run with all my Brockton friends, not just the ones who became pros. I can tell that Zoe is struggling a bit with the news. She's happy for me but wishes she was pregnant too. I don't think they've been trying for very long, but the girl has never been particularly patient when she decides she wants something.

Jim is excited for us but I think a little freaked out that he's old enough to be a grandfather. He's only in his forties, and having been a bachelor most of his life, he lives a little differently than most guys his age. I can see Jace's pride at the growing family echoed in Jim's eyes though, and I know he won't have any trouble with the grandpa role. He's already talking about converting Jace's downstairs space in his house into an epic playroom involving knocking down Jace's old bedroom. He's in the construction business and has seen some Pinter-est-worthy playrooms over the years, so he inundates us with his ideas. That's how Jim shows excitement and love, through projects. Jace and I decide not to remind him that it will be a while before Baby Wilder actually needs a playroom.

There hasn't been any follow-up from the gossip article, and it blew right over. I'm sure Drake meant for it to stir up a shitstorm either in our marriage or in the media, but when we didn't react, no one paid much attention to it. I've been holding off on speaking with Coach Harding about running with him. I wanted things to settle a bit, and make sure that the gossip about Ryan didn't escalate. Now, I'm back in his office at the field house, remembering that very first meeting I had with him as a college freshman. I was still trying to find my place on the team back then, and now I'm so much more confident in my running career, my potential. Ironically, even though it's my profession, I'm less uptight about it too. I know that hard work pays off eventually; if not in this season, down the road it will.

Ryan's dad congratulates me on the baby off the bat and then tells me how great it's been for his small group of pros to have me join them these past few months. "I know that Lexi and Sienna really benefitted from having you join on some of those harder training runs, Pep."

"That's actually what I wanted to talk to you about, Coach." He's told me to call him Mark but I don't know if I'll ever be able to stop calling him Coach. "I left the Newbound team."

Coach Harding doesn't look surprised. "I know. I spoke with Ray a few days ago. That was a good decision."

Frowning, I shift forward in my chair. "Why do you say that?" When I was considering my options as a college senior, Coach helped me get connected with Ray, touting him as the top marathon coach, particularly for women with Monica Herrick as his protégée.

Coach's eyes dart away and he hesitates. "A press release is coming out tomorrow about this. Monica Herrick tested positive for doping."

My jaw drops. I stare at Coach, speechless. The greatest female distance runner in the country for the past decade, my teammate for the first couple of years of my professional career, is about to be outed for doping? You've got to be shitting me.

Coach sighs. "I don't know if Ray knew, but it's awfully hard for me to believe he didn't at least have suspicions. Based on what he told me, the evidence is fairly decisive. You know there's often a gray area in these situations, but this is actually her second positive test in as many years. The first one was swept under the rug. Which, from what I understand, Ray had a hand in."

I shake my head. "How could I not know anything about this? I did a training block with them last August. I just saw Monica and some of our other teammates at the 10K in Boston two months ago."

"You're the only runner on Newbound not based in Arizona. The other runners on the team are all going to be scrutinized very closely. You probably will be too." Mark gives me a sympathetic look. "I hope your name isn't swept into this and tainted with doubts. The good news is that you mostly trained solo. People might take a close look at your debut half though and wonder how you ran so fast pregnant. I think you'll need to be prepared for that."

My heart rate picks up as I take in what he's saying. He's right. I was going to wait until the twelve-week mark to announce my pregnancy publicly, but I may need to do it a couple of weeks early. "I have all my blood tests from two days after that race," I tell Coach Harding. "Will that clear me?" Panic invades my question. Once there's suspicion surrounding an athlete, it never goes away completely. My entire career could be ruined. As my chest squeezes at this possibility, a bubble of hysterics threatens to break loose. A moment ago I sat here cool as a cucumber thinking how much more I had it together since my freshman year. And now I'm about to lose it. I try desperately to latch on to the confidence that it will all work out as long as I stay true to my training and my values.

Coach Harding stands up and comes over to the other side of his desk, sitting on the edge. "Pepper, I'll do whatever I can to help keep your name out of this. Yes, let's get those blood samples sent to USADA before they even ask, to get ahead of the game. Then let's work with your publicist to put the best spin possible on this. Explain you left the team weeks ago before you even knew about what was going on, that you wanted to train here in Brockton because the coaching style wasn't working for you. That will imply you weren't totally okay with Ray's methods."

"I wasn't. He assumed I'd –" I suck in a harsh breath before quickly letting the rest tumble out, "have an abortion."

When Coach Harding sucks in his own breath right behind me, the tightness in my chest eases just a bit. He understands how hard that hit. He gets it.

"Your instincts to leave that team were right. From our few conversations since you've graduated, I sensed you weren't clicking entirely with Ray or the women on his team. I wanted to offer for you to join us but I wanted to give you more time before putting that in front of you. I also was hoping to recruit a couple more women who could train with you. Lexi and Sienna are close, but I think you would really benefit from one or two female training partners who will challenge and push you. I'm working on bringing some on to the team."

"So, I can join your group?"

Coach Harding smiles. "Of course. That's what I'm saying. That's what you came here today to talk to me about, right?" I nod and his smile widens. "We'd love to have you. Now, as you know, Ryan does a lot of the day to day coaching at workouts and check-ins. With the college team, I simply can't be present at workouts and races very often. But you know Ryan's grown up being inundated with my training philosophies and he's really got excellent intuition."

He's not wrong. Ryan's always been wise beyond his years when it comes to everything running-related.

"I know. Obviously, I won't be training seriously again for a little while, so there's no rush in recruiting more training partners for me specifically or figuring out all the details."

"Exactly. Now, let's talk about your plan while pregnant. I remember when Marie went through that with Ryan. Based on her experience and others I've spoken with, I think you should take it day by day, and have no expectations on your body running-wise during this time."

Another knot of tension releases at his words. This is the approach that felt right to me all along. I had wondered if he'd have the same ideas as Ray about continuing to maintain a high level of intense training all the way through with the goal of hitting the ground, well, running, in every sense of the word as soon as the baby was born. Of course, I'd forgotten I had a resource right here in Ryan's mom, a former professional runner.

"I like that plan. I've felt great, to be honest. It's surprising really. But I don't need the pressure to keep up a certain level of fitness, and I really want to be able to back off if anything feels off, and not have to feel guilty about it."

"That's wonderful you've felt great, Pepper. Marie had a rough go of it first trimester with both boys." Conversation switches to Ryan's younger brother, Kevin, who is now a runner at UC on his dad's team.

Despite the devastating news about Monica and the scrutiny I'll be under as a result, I feel renewed and clear-headed when I leave Coach Harding's office. Things really are coming together. As I walk to my car, I'm surprised by a sharp tightening low in my belly. It takes my breath away for a moment, and I pause in the parking lot.

The last couple of days I've had stomachaches, and I've been debating calling Dr. Burch to ask if it's normal. I've already called her with so many random questions, I'm trying to hold out until the twelve-week ultrasound coming up. I haven't told Jace, because I know he'll worry, but it seems strange to have stomachaches like this without nausea. I haven't felt any morning sickness, and now suddenly I'm getting cramps.

The pain usually only lasts a few minutes, but it's still cramping by the time I get back to Gran's. I don't even realize tears are running down my face until I rush in the front door and Jace looks up from the couch, where he's studying old football videos. He takes one look at me, and we both know something isn't right.

Chapter Seventeen

JACE

When Pepper stormed into the house, cheeks wet, skin ashen, I think I already knew what had happened. My heart knew because it stopped beating for a few seconds. But I had to be strong for Pepper so I rushed to her, picked her up and tried to comprehend what was going on.

"My stomach," she gasped, clutching it. "The baby."

It took all my control to maintain an outward calm. "Let's go to the hospital. I'm going to drive us there, okay?"

"I think I'm bleeding," she said through gasps for breath. I couldn't tell if the sobs shaking her body were from physical or emotional pain. "Take me to the bathroom."

As much as I wanted to drive directly to the hospital, I couldn't deny my wife's request when she was in this state. I stayed with her while she tried to pull down her leggings. Pepper's hands were shaking hard, clammy to the touch when I took them in mine before slowly easing the leggings down to her ankles. The panties came next, and we both stopped breathing when we saw what was between her legs. Blood. It wasn't everywhere, but it wasn't the light spotting she'd had a week ago that Dr. Burch said was normal.

It took all my concentration to push my emotions back while I found clean panties and sweats for Pepper to change into. But she refused to put them on, shaking her head violently as she pulled the bloodied ones back up her legs. I swallowed hard at what she'd done. I understood why she didn't want to throw them in the hamper with the rest of the dirty laundry, and I tried not to choke on the sob that wanted to come out of my own lungs. Instead, I scooped her up again and carried her to my old Jeep, parked in my dad's driveway. I buckled her in and we drove to the Brockton Community Hospital in devastated silence.

When we arrived, they told us what we already knew. Pepper, who had settled into numbness until that moment, broke into another round of sobs. We held each other like that, her in a hospital gown, clutching the bloody panties and leggings to her chest, and me holding onto her with all I had left in me.

The blur of loss was thick and the air tasted like dust for hours even after we left the hospital and returned home. Pepper went straight to our room and I tucked her into bed. I wanted to crawl in behind her but I needed to be the one to handle sharing the news. Of course, I probably didn't have to say anything to Bunny. She knew immediately what had happened when she saw me carrying Pepper inside.

My voice came out as a croak when I told her, "We lost Baby Wilder." Gran opened her little arms and took me into her chest, enveloping me in her love. Damn it felt good to be loved by this lady. I let out the tears I'd held in until I was wrung dry. The grief wasn't gone, but I was clear-headed when I pulled away minutes later.

"A miscarriage. Nothing unusual or complicated. Just a ten-week miscarriage," I repeated what I knew. Saying the diagnosis like that, it sounded so insignificant, something that happened all the time. Standard. Nothing to dwell on. But we'd lost a baby. Yeah, the baby hadn't been born yet but it was still a death. All that hope and love we had wrapped around the baby was lost. A baby we hadn't planned for and didn't know how badly we wanted, yet I knew that both of us would hurt from this for a long while. The pain was intense, and while I knew from experience that pain lessened with time, I also knew that some pains never fully went away. They stayed with you forever.

Chapter Eighteen

PEPPER

It hurts. The ER doctor told me that my stomach might continue to cramp for a day or two, but that pain was nothing compared to the pain everywhere else in my body. My limbs. My head. Mostly, it came directly from my heart, radiating through my lungs and infecting my entire body with a weight so heavy I didn't know if I'd ever get out of bed again. At least not on my own. I don't know how much time passed but Jace has been carrying me to the bathroom, brushing my teeth, trying to get me to eat and drink; he even threw me in the shower at one point. Well, he didn't *throw* me. He stood with me and washed me like I was a little kid. The pain was so strong I couldn't even speak.

I don't understand it. I hadn't even wanted a baby. Or at least, I hadn't known I'd wanted a baby. But this little life in me had changed everything about how I thought of my life, my career, my hopes and dreams. It had all been rearranged, and was reassembling with renewed purpose. And Little Wilder is just gone. I feel broken now. I can't go back to who I was before.

JACE

One day of despondency turned into three, and now it had been a week and I was fucking losing my mind with worry. Gran wasn't holding up much better. She'd been the one to tell me to give Pepper time, but now she was pacing in the hallway outside our room, wringing her hands. Our own grief for the loss had dropped significantly in priority as Pepper sunk into a kind of depression neither of us knew she was capable of. She was the bright, optimistic one in the house most of the time. Serious and disciplined when necessary, but always ready to bounce back from disappointment, determined to chase the next goal.

I'd been ready for anything from her – to tell me she wanted to try again immediately or wait years – to beg to stay in Brockton or move far away – to quit running or dive back into it with a vengeance. But this? Complete despondency? This I couldn't have prepared myself for. This I didn't think I could handle. It gutted me.

While Pepper lay in bed for a week straight, a media storm had hit with positive drug test results for Monica Herrick, the star runner on Newbound. I'd begun fielding calls and emails on Pepper's phone, and confided in Ryan's dad, Mark Harding, of all people. When I told him what happened after he left her office on Friday, he helped me coordinate with Pepper's publicist about a statement, get the results from her blood test confirming the story that she'd separated from Newbound weeks before this occurred after learning she was pregnant. In the same statement, we had to confirm the miscarriage as well, which would hopefully create sympathy rather than suspicion. Pepper would hate to use the miscarriage to her advantage like that, but I didn't see it that way. We were just telling the story honestly and openly to avoid getting her name and reputation dragged through the mud with Ray and Monica and the other Newbound runners.

I'd tried to consult Pepper about all of this but she'd stared into space blankly. I'd needed her consent on the medical records and approval of the press release, and she typed the words and signed her name where I asked, but I was torn. I needed to deal with all this but I didn't think she'd actually processed anything I'd told her.

I didn't want to bombard her with all this shit right now. In the end, I trusted Mark because Pepper trusted him. He told me they'd discussed the situation and how to handle it and that she'd been on board with this open approach before. Before the miscarriage. But that was before she lost the baby, when she was excited and happy to tell the world about the pregnancy. Would she still want that?

I wasn't sure, but I knew that the consequences could be grave if we didn't get a statement out soon. Silence was often construed as guilt, and once speculation started to brew, it was already too late. So I pulled the trigger, and gave the nod, through Pepper's "consent" for the statements in the press release, with her story of what happened, and her blood test results. I was quoted as well, saying that we were grieving the loss and to stay the fuck away. The publicist modified the words a little but it got the message across.

Bunny huffed out a big breath and announced she was going in. She opened the door and marched to Pepper's side of the bed, sitting in the armchair we'd moved over there to try to talk to her and force food into her the past few days.

I opened the blinds partway to let in some light and then sat down on the other side of the bed. I needed to touch her somehow, to have some connection, so I brushed hair away from her forehead. Her eyes were open, staring ahead blindly, her hands tucked under her cheek. She was curled up in a ball under the covers.

"Pepper Jones Wilder. It's been one week. You have not left this room." Bunny was trying to use a firm voice but wasn't very successful. Empathy dripped with every word, and I could practically hear her heart breaking for her granddaughter as she watched her frail body.

"I made chicken dumpling soup. Your favorite Pillsbury crescent rolls. And lemon meringue pie. You're going to take a bath, get dressed and join us for dinner. Then you'll sit on the couch and watch a movie. Then you can go back to your hideout until breakfast. But we're going to keep moving forward. We won't let you stay here forever."

When Pepper didn't respond, I saw Bunny's lower lip tremble. Before she broke down, she darted out of the room. Shit. Now I had two distraught women to take care of.

I lifted the covers and slid underneath. She didn't react when I pulled her body to mine, her back to my front.

"Please talk to me, baby. Anything. Just tell me what you're feeling."

Silence.

I kept running my hands over her legs, hips, arms, kissing her neck and cheek. I wasn't trying to start anything, I just wanted any reaction. A sign she was actually here with me.

Finally, she spoke. "Where are the underwear?" she asked.

My hands froze. Another round of bleeding had soaked a second pair of underwear the next day. She'd allowed me to take them off her for a shower, but had grabbed them from me when I'd tried to take them to wash. Both bloodied pairs had been on the floor next to our bed all week. I'd finally let Bunny take them this morning while Pepper was sleeping.

"We washed them," I told her. "They're in the dryer." I'd almost thrown them out, but now I was grateful I'd had the foresight not to. Pepper had attached Baby Wilder to those underwear, and in a way, she wasn't wrong. The blood did represent the baby's life. Putting the panties in the trash would have broken her. Maybe it was too late for that. She was broken already, a week later clinging to the only tangible connection she felt to the baby. I didn't know how to fix her, except to be here.

I heard her crying softly. "I know it doesn't make sense," she said. She was referring to the panties still, and the new round of grief she felt at them going through the washing machine.

I hushed her and tried to tell her it was okay. I was surprised when she let me take her into a bath, and then when she asked me to come in with her. It was a small bathtub for two adults, but I couldn't say no. "I don't want to be alone. It hurts so much."

Finally, she was at least talking. "I know, Pep."

Frankie and Lizzie's wedding was tomorrow. I didn't know if I should tell her or not. With everything going on in the media about her running, and Drake trying to stir up a story about exes, I didn't want to go to the wedding without her. But I was a groomsman, and I couldn't stand them up.

It was strange sitting in a bathtub with my wife and being unable to touch her sexually. I knew instinctually that even though her body might be recovered already, her mind needed more time. Pepper's pain hurt me almost worse than the loss that caused it. Both were out of my control.

"It's going to take time, but it will start to hurt less. I promise."

"You can't promise that," she whispered.

I didn't want to tell her this now, but I needed to give her something good to hold onto. "I signed a contract with the Stallions yesterday, baby. We're staying in Brockton."

She was nestled between my legs in the tub and I couldn't see her expression. I wish I could. Maybe there would finally be some life there. Some hope. She took my hand in hers and squeezed it gently. That was enough. Enough to tell me that it would take time. But she'd be okay. We'd be okay.

Chapter Nineteen

PEPPER

My first time leaving the house in over a week and we're going to a wedding with hundreds of people. Jace is in the wedding, and I'm grateful that Gran and Wallace were invited too. I can sit with them during the ceremony, and maybe I can use them as an excuse not to be social. Normally that wouldn't be an option with Gran, but she's watching me like a hawk, rubbing my back every few seconds, and patting me on the shoulder. "You look absolutely beautiful. But you need to eat at least three pieces of wedding cake tonight. You're too skinny."

I'm used to Gran trying to beef me up with sweets, but this time, she sounds more serious than usual. After glancing briefly in the bathroom mirror earlier, I understood where she was coming from. My cheekbones stood out too much, my skin was pasty, and dark circles hung under my eyes. One week without fresh air or food did not look good on me.

It shocked me when Gran came to tell me that I'd been in bed a full week. An entire week without leaving the bedroom. I *really* didn't want to. I wanted to rest in the pain, leave it sitting right there with me. I was scared that if I left the room, the pain would stab twice as hard and knock the breath out of me again. I was also scared that the pain would dull, and I'd be leaving Baby Wilder behind. Moving on. I didn't want to move on. But I got up and did it anyway. For Jace. For Gran.

It was hard enough sitting through a huge dinner and a movie. It felt like being under bright lights after years in a dungeon. The analogy wasn't too far off from the truth. But now, going to a wedding? There isn't even a comparable analogy. It's a huge leap. I'm fighting between numbness and excruciating pain in my heart. No one's making me go. But I don't want to be alone with a babysitter. Okay, Lulu and Harold or Jim wouldn't be strangers and I wouldn't be alone, but being separated from Jace for hours makes me feel sick. Which is silly. Until recently we were separated all the time.

I take a deep breath and shake my head. My world is upside-down. But I need to face it. I'm a fragile shell of who I was a week ago, but I can't stay this way forever.

JACE

Pepper was surprisingly composed when we got to the wedding venue. It was in Lizzie's hometown, at her grandparents' ranch, about a forty-minute drive east of Brockton. Pepper was distant, but not despondent. I was a mess. Frankie and Lizzie knew what was going on and told me not to worry about showing for the pre-ceremony shit with the other groomsmen. There were going to be a ton of people here from UC, a ton of people who were still living in or near Brockton. Most would have heard about the pregnancy, some would have heard about the miscarriage too. The press release with the whole story went out this morning, including to the local Brockton news, but I didn't know if everyone would have heard. And if they had, I couldn't imagine anyone would understand. Few of our friends were married or had kids. I didn't know of anyone who'd had a miscarriage. Maybe they did and I just didn't know, but still. I couldn't trust people to be tactful about it, especially if they didn't get it. What if someone congratulated Pepper about being pregnant because they didn't know about the miscarriage? What if someone thought she didn't want it anyway and brushed it off, saying it was for the best? Fuck.

When I parked, Gran told me to stay in the car. Wallace got out from the passenger side and opened Pepper's door. Pepper was operating like a robot at that moment, so she took Wallace's hand and let him help her out of the car. She was simply stunning in a clingy dress with swirls of teal and tan. A little bonier than usual, a bit too pale, but still breathtaking. I wanted my wife healthy again. Seeing her like this was tearing me up.

"Jace Vernon Wilder," Gran said from behind me. She'd scooted up in her seat and poked her head through the space between the two front seats. Bunny was torn up too, but she was back to channeling her inner tough-girl attitude.

"Bernadette," I replied through the lump in my throat.

"You were white-knuckling the steering wheel." She called me out.

"This was a bad idea. People are going to bombard her. She's so fragile, Buns. What if she's not ready? What if this breaks her more?" Was that even possible? What would that look like? "Fuck." I slammed a frustrated fist into the steering wheel.

"Jace. This needs to run its course. But we also have to get her out of the house. If she missed this wedding, she'd be upset. Maybe not right away, but she would be. She needs to be here. You can't protect her from the world, Jace. You know this. You have to let her live. People will say the wrong things." I cringed at the reality. "They will. Pepper is strong. She's dealt with people saying the wrong things for a long time, with you as her guy," Bunny reminded me with a knowing tilt of her head. "She'll be just fine."

I nodded. "I know. It fucking hurts to know how bad she hurts," I admitted, needing to unload it on someone. Gran nodded too, knowing exactly how I felt.

"Let's drink some bourbon. It's a bourbon kind of night and Frankie told me they'd have a yummy selection. Wallace will drive us home."

I got out and held Pepper close as we walked to an old barn. The view of the Rocky Mountains from out here was unreal. In Brockton, the view of the foothills wasn't as dramatic. Beautiful, yes, but not nearly as breathtaking as the snowcapped mountains far off in the distance from the plains. I glanced at Pepper and saw her taking it in. She registered the beauty and that gave me hope. When she squeezed my hand, I decided we'd done the right thing coming tonight. I wanted my Pepper back. People could be insensitive, and they would be, but we already knew it was a cruel world at times. At least we had each other and our family of close friends in Brockton. At least Brockton would be home again, for the long-term.

Turned out I didn't need to worry. Though the press release announcing my trade to the Stallions wasn't coming until Monday, the news had spread like wildfire. I'd told Frankie two days ago that I'd be signing the final version the next day. With everything going on for the wedding, I doubted he was the one to spread the word. It could have been the coaches, an agent who caught wind, an assistant — it wasn't something we were keeping too hushed. After all, I wasn't playing around, pitting teams against each other to get the biggest deal. As soon as I'd dropped Drake from involvement, I'd gone straight to the Stallions and told them to get it done. People were more interested in the news of me joining the team than they were about our personal life, or at least, it gave them something else to talk about with me that wasn't painful.

I'd watched Pepper throughout the ceremony, sandwiched between Bunny and Angel. She was there, but she wasn't. I wanted to gather her up, shake life back into her somehow, but I knew I had to be patient. I fucking sucked at patience.

After the ceremony, there were pictures with the wedding party, and then some with friends. I didn't know if Pepper managed to turn her lips up in a smile for the photographer, but she stood there beside me and endured it. Throughout cocktail hour, I sensed the attention circling us. I was used to being the center focus at social gatherings, that was just our reality, but tonight it made me uneasy. This party was filled with NFL players and supermodels, which already should have dispersed some of the attention. Sure, we were new, the rumors of me joining the team fresh, but this was Frankie and Lizzie's wedding. People should be focused on them. It pissed me off.

A waiter came by with champagne and I contemplated snagging

one for Pepper. She might sip on some bubbly if it was in her hand, just to go with the flow. I could tell she was in robot mode, going through the motions. Maybe a little alcohol would help? Bunny made the decision for us when she bustled over with a tray of glasses filled with amber liquid. She placed it on the high-top table beside us.

"Wallace wanted to stay to hit on the bartender. She's got big—" Bunny made circle motions by her chest and gave us wide eyes.

Wallace shrugged. "I was just being a gentleman. Ain't easy running an open bar with all these hooligan kids around."

Pepper's stance at my side softened, and I was grateful the banter was calming her a bit. Bunny handed us each a glass and raised hers in the air. "To marriage."

Pepper, who hadn't uttered a word since we arrived, repeated the toast along with me before taking a tentative sip. Bunny winked at me as we threw ours back.

When I saw Stephanie Bremer eyeing us, I quickly looked away. I didn't want to give her an opening to come over here. She'd rubbed me the wrong way both times I'd interacted with her. But it was too late; a moment later, she appeared with Troy at her side.

Ignoring Bunny and Wallace, she greeted us with the same border-line-inappropriately familiar hugs and exuberance she did at Frankie's fundraiser back in February.

Troy congratulated me with a handshake on joining the team but didn't say more. It'd be nice if he'd acknowledge I'd been hired to fill his shoes; it would ease some awkwardness and tension. He hadn't officially announced this was his last season, but everyone knew it.

Stephanie zeroed in on Pepper and my spine straightened. "Boy, a lot has changed for the two of you since we saw you, what? Less than four months ago. I'm so sorry to hear about your loss," she said, without an ounce of sincerity. I pulled Pepper closer to me, wishing I could stop whatever was going to escape Stephanie's lips next. "Don't worry, sweetie." She patted Pepper on the arm, and Pepper went rigid against me. "At least it was early on. You'll have another. Well, if you stop running so much maybe you will. I'm sure that didn't help. Now that you're ready for family life, you can stick by your husband's side like we talked about, hmm?"

My fists clenched and for the first time in my life, I had an urge to punch a woman. I'd met some awful women, but what she just said would stab my wife right in the gut when she had no shields up to protect herself. It was going to be irreversible.

Chapter Twenty

PEPPER

It's like a bucket of ice has been dumped on my head. A heavy one. Because it shocks and freezes me, but it hurts too. I sense Jace shift beside me and expect him to lash out somehow, since I'm incapable of a retort. Instead, Gran steps from behind Troy. The Bremers blocked out Wallace and Gran when they entered our space, but Gran's not having it. I've never seen her look so pissed in all our lives. Her face is red, eyes blazing. And then her hand reaches out and slaps Stephanie right across the cheek. As Stephanie sputters in outrage, Wallace snags a glass of champagne from a passing waiter and calmly nudges a stunned Troy Bremer to the side to dump it on Stephanie's head.

Stephanie's mouth is open in shock and Troy tries to soothe her with a pat on her back, urging her to go to the ladies' to freshen up. He doesn't defend her, and he even looks a little bit smug, or possibly amused, I can't tell which.

"How dare you! Who do you think you are? Who are these people?" She's screaming, gesturing wildly at Wallace and Bunny.

Bunny gets on her tiptoes and points a little finger at her. "I'm Pepper's gran, Bernadette Jones. And this is my husband, Wallace. And I already know who you are. And I don't care. I don't *tolerate* no one talking to Pepper like that." Gran looks ready to say more but Wallace places a hand on her lower back and she calms.

I notice the chatter around us has stopped, and everyone is staring in fascination. No one comes to Stephanie's rescue and her husband manages to drag her away, taking advantage of her state of disbelief.

I've been shocked right back into reality.

The Walkers and the Snyders join us a moment later, Angel and Leah clapping lightly. "I've been wanting to do that for years. Don't know what prompted it, but I have no doubt she deserved it," Angel declares with a wink in Wallace and Gran's direction. "I'm Angel Walker, this is my husband Tanner."

Bunny shakes herself and engages in introductions all around with the Snyders too. Jace's hold hasn't loosened around me. Actually, he's holding me so tightly I can barely breathe. Wallace raises his hand. "I think more drinks are in order after that ordeal." He marches toward the bar.

Gran watches him go. "He was just looking for an excuse to flirt with the bartender. Got his wish."

"Her boobs are huge," Angel loud-whispers. Leah giggles and blushes.

We sat by them at the ceremony, and they said they were sorry and also congratulations for joining the Stallions. I acted weird, I know I did. I think I just kind of grimaced at them. I was scared if I spoke, I'd start crying, so I just didn't say anything. Now, I'm just thankful they aren't avoiding us. Even if I'm not ready to act normally, I still want everyone else to act normally around me. Which really doesn't make much sense, but not much does at the moment.

As Gran makes new friends with the Walkers and the Snyders, Jace remains frozen, his arms squeezing me tight. He knows I'm internalizing every word Stephanie said. Letting it eat away at me, turn me inside out. She's voiced exactly what was lying just beneath the surface of the paralyzing pain. As soon as I broke through that, I'm facing an onslaught of new emotions. And these ones might hurt worse. Guilt, self-loathing, and a new kind of grief for the loss of running. Will I ever find joy in it again? It feels tainted. Racing an Olympic Trials qualifying time while seven weeks pregnant? Of course that's what killed Baby Wilder. And then I didn't even stop. I kept running. Not hard, but I know that it was my fault. My selfishness to do what I love, even when my body couldn't take it. Sure it wasn't hurting these past few weeks, but I fainted. That should have told me everything I needed to know. Baby Wilder didn't want me to run.

We're at an assigned table with some of the wedding party for dinner, and I simply can't engage. People try to bring me into the conversation, but I can hardly process what they're asking me. It's all a dull buzzing noise around me as my head seeks that dark numbness it's been in all week. Not numbness exactly, the pain doesn't go away, but it's safer than facing all these happy, boisterous people.

As soon as the speeches are over, Jace takes my hand and tugs me through the tables, all the way out of the barn into the dark night.

He places two sturdy palms on my shoulders. "Pepper, talk to me." His voice breaks as his eyes search mine, and he pleads, "Please."

I shake my head, unwilling to do this. Not here, not now. Not ever. I don't want him to placate me. He's not a doctor. He doesn't know. I need to be here in this dark place alone. I deserve the self-hatred I'm inflicting on myself. But even as I think that, watching Jace suffer breaks something else inside me, and before I know it, my lower lip is trembling with the effort not to cry.

I don't say anything, but he knows. He knows exactly what I'm thinking and feeling and he won't let me suffer alone. Jace shakes his head. "No, Pep. You are *not* blaming yourself for this. This can happen for all kinds of reasons out of your control, and it was weeks after you raced. It came on out of nowhere." Jace shakes me as he speaks, enunciating each word with urgency. He's trying to get through to me, but I don't want to let him in.

"The ER doc said it was most likely spontaneous. Not from a traumatic event. It was not. Your. Fault."

Tears stream down my face. It *was* my fault. "Jace. You're wrong. I traumatized the baby when I raced. I got so dehydrated I fainted. If I hadn't done that," I gasp for breath and my hand goes to my stomach, "we'd still have a baby," I finish quietly. "So don't tell me something that's not true."

Jace drops his hands from my shoulders and glares at me, begging me to see it his way. I glare right back.

I don't know how long we stand there, me with tears drying on my face, Jace standing a foot away, looking furious. He's right there in front of me but could be miles away. There's a party with hundreds of people on the other side of the door, yet I've never felt so alone.

A couple stumbles out the door, breaking the silent battle. The girl giggles as the guy throws an arm around her, mumbling about a gazebo they can go to. I don't know them but when they spot us, there's recognition in their eyes.

"Oh, hey man," the guy says, straightening up and nodding at Jace. "Everything okay?"

Does it look like it? I want to shout. I'm crying, we're not touching. *Keep moving, buddy.*

I'm angry at their carefree attitudes, their flirtations, the way they seem to be enjoying each other and having fun. It feels like I'll never go back to that place again. It feels so very far away. Irrelevant.

Jace juts out his chin. "Hey. Fine."

The guy gets the hint and the girl ducks her head as they walk quickly in the direction of the gazebo or wherever to get away from us and back to their flirty cocoon. I hear the girl ask, "That's Pepper and Jace Wilder, right?"

When I see Jace's taut body sag, his shoulders slumping, I relax. I shouldn't be relieved at his defeat. I *should* be feeling something for his own pain. He can't control this situation and that's killing him. Normally I'd try to console him, but I just can't. He doesn't understand the weight I'm carrying on my chest right now. The grief and anger directed inward. There's no room for empathy, no space to feel anything outside myself. I barely registered the joy filling the air at the ceremony. Hardly processed fury toward Stephanie for being a bitch. Gran and Wallace's throwdown should have done more than caused me to evaluate everyone else's reaction. I should have been amused, embarrassed, grateful. It's like I'm an outsider, recognizing what *should* be happening, but unable to fully experience it firsthand.

When I shiver from the slight chill outside, Jace places a firm hand on my back and leads me inside again. I play my part, eating cake, dancing, hugging Frankie and Lizzie with a smile on my face, and keeping clear of the Bremers to avoid further drama.

Jace does not leave my side. He even hovers outside the ladies' room when I'm in there. Despite the emotional distance between us, I find I need him close by. I don't understand it, but his presence keeps me from unraveling. Helps me maintain the façade. Right, I'm not doing the best job at pretending, but at least I'm here, interacting somewhat normally without crying at every turn. It feels like a real feat.

When we get home, I sit on the bed and watch Jace take off his tux. It's a monumental tease seeing him undress in our bedroom, and the guilt in my heart only intensifies as heat stirs in my belly. The man is simply too handsome, too perfectly sculpted, and his love for me is too flawless. I've never been more broken than I am right now, yet he still looks at me with adoration. Frustration too, but he's trying to be patient. Will I break him down? Will I destroy the way he loves me, or will it destroy him first? I know that it can't end any other way but with more pain. I don't see how we can go back to being like that couple headed to the gazebo, nothing but hope ahead of us.

Jace is standing in his boxer briefs, taking in the confusion and lust I'm sure is radiating from me in waves. The crease between his brows and bulge under his briefs tells me he feels the same way. I swallow. "I'm not ready." I don't know how to tell him that I don't know if I ever will be. How can I explain to the man who loves me that I don't feel like I deserve his lovemaking? That I don't deserve the chance of more Wilder babies, that even as I'm hot with need, the idea of doing the very act that led us to this heartbreak sends panic and maybe even disgust right through me?

Jace's eyes close briefly. I can't read him right now. Is he angry? Sad? Annoyed? Disappointed? He walks toward me and crouches in front of me. He slides one cowboy boot off my foot, then the other. His eyes remain on my legs as his hands run from my ankle all the way up to my hips. My breath hitches when he starts to pull my underwear down. Lifting my hips, I keep my eyes on him, trying to figure out what he's doing. He's being so damn gentle, and it's wearing me down. Is that his intent?

He gets off the ground, but only to come around and place his knees behind me, unzipping the back of my dress and letting it fall to my waist. He pauses, and the only sound is our ragged breathing. I wish more than anything I wasn't so turned on right now. I'm putty, each brush of his fingertips like a jolt straight to my core. When he unclasps my bra, freeing my breasts, the air on my skin alone makes me shudder. Lips brush my shoulder, then the spot under my ear, and I almost moan.

"I'll get your pajamas," he whispers.

Oh. Okay, he wasn't trying to work me up. Well, he damn well did. Jace hops off the bed, finds clean boy shorts and a soft tee in my drawer and tosses them to me. Gentle attentive Jace is gone as he goes to his own dresser to pull off his underwear and put on a fresh pair. He's turned sideways from me, but I don't miss the angry hard-on jutting from his body. I grimace. It looks painful.

If I can't let him love me how he wants to, and I can't let him in emotionally, at least I can give him some relief. I stand up, letting the dress fall all the way to the floor, and walk to him fully naked. My hand reaches for his wrist to stop him from putting on new boxer briefs.

When I drop to my knees, Jace tries to protest. "Pepper, you don't have to do that." Yeah, he definitely sounds like a guy in agony.

"Let me, Jace. It's all I can give you right now." When my mouth touches him, he can't stop me. Jace leans his frame against the wall with a sigh of relief as I take him. I try to ignore the pulsing between my own legs as I pleasure my husband, but it's not easy. It doesn't take long for Jace to come in my mouth, and when I taste him deep in my throat, I have to battle my own release threatening to erupt. Simply by having this connection after nearly two weeks without it, I'm on fire. But I can't give in. Instead, I relish my own physical distress as I slip into my sleep clothes, brush my teeth, and climb into bed.

When Jace reaches for me under the covers, I take his hand and stop it from traveling lower. I've felt entirely too much as it is tonight. I need him beside me, but I can't handle that kind of touch.

Chapter Twenty-One

JACE

Pepper retreated back into herself after the wedding. She came out of her room to eat meals, if a few bites here and there counted, and then went back to bed. I was about ready to lose my fucking mind. I'd asked Lexi and Zoe to come over to talk to her, to try to get her out of the house, on a walk, anything. They'd returned a few times to try to hang out with her but she'd barely engaged. Then I tried Coach Harding, and had the same response. I was tempted to cycle all of her friends, from Wes to Jenny Mendoza, maybe even Ryan. I was desperate. My wife was in a deep depression and I didn't know how to pull her out of it. Another week had passed since the wedding without her leaving the house.

As I hovered over Pep, pulling my hair out with helplessness, my dad was trying to get *me* out of the house. He said I couldn't be there for Pepper if I was a mess myself, but I couldn't leave her. We were connected by the same loss, like a cord, and however tenuous, I had this feeling that she'd know if I went further than one room over from her. That me being close was absolutely necessary to Pepper's well-being. It was a strange, visceral sensation, almost like it was straight out of some supernatural movie, where we'd get sick if we were too far apart. Wasn't that in some movie? Shit. Maybe I was starting to lose it.

Maybe Dad was right and I needed to get outside, get some exercise, do something besides pace.

I'd been fielding Pep's calls and when I saw Dr. Burch's office calling, I hurried out of the bedroom to answer. It was a nurse.

"Is Ms. Wilder available, please?"

"Um, actually, this is her husband, Jace Wilder. Is there something I can help you with?" I asked. I heard the nurse shuffling around some papers.

"Ah, Jace Wilder. Yes. Pepper listed you as someone we can share her medical information with."

I held my breath as I waited for her to get to the point.

"Pepper missed her ultrasound appointment today. It was at one o'clock. We can try to reschedule the appointment later this week."

Thank fuck Pepper didn't answer the phone. "That won't be necessary. Pepper had a miscarriage a little over two weeks ago. One of us should have notified your office, canceled the appointment, but..." Neither one of us were in a state to do it after the ER visit, and then it didn't even occur to me. Of course, the ER isn't connected to the OBGYN office, so they never would have known.

"Oh dear. I'm so sorry for your loss. Dr. Burch will want to see Pepper to follow up. Is she available to make an appointment?"

"Uh, actually, Pepper's not doing so well. She hasn't left the house since this happened. Except for a wedding. She won't run, hardly eats, and won't, um, do anything else that makes her happy. Can Dr. Burch maybe recommend someone she can see for depression in this situation?" I was uneasy sharing this information with a stranger, but I was desperate. Pepper needed help beyond what I could give her.

The nurse squeezed Pepper into Dr. Burch's schedule the next day, telling me that Dr. Burch would evaluate her before referring her to someone else. I hoped I could get Pepper to the appointment. When I turned back down the hallway, I found Pepper standing in the doorway to our bedroom.

"We missed the ultrasound, didn't we?" she asked.

Shit. I walked quickly to her, not bothering to answer.

Pepper fell into my arms, and I caught her. She hadn't cried since Saturday night but a dam burst open in that moment. "It hurts. It hurts so bad," she said, sobbing into my chest. My heart broke for her as I rubbed her back, wishing I could make it all go away.

"I know. I know, Pep."

I let her cry for minutes, until her body grew weak in my arms, and she didn't have any tears left in her.

"I heard what you said." She pulled back, wiping her cheeks with the sleeves of one of my old sweatshirts. "That I need help."

When I started to respond she shook her head. "No, you're right. I can't keep going like this. I don't know what to do. But I know I need to try. For you. For us. For Gran. I can't stay in here forever." She sniffled and let out a half-hearted chuckle. "I want to, but that's not living. And I need to figure out how to start living again."

Her admission nearly made my knees buckle with relief. If she could see this much, there was hope she'd come back to me.

"But I want you to come with me to see someone. I don't want to talk to some stranger about everything without you there, too. When do you have to travel again?"

I blinked in confusion. "I'm not traveling anymore. Well, not until our first away game in September, almost four months from now."

She let out a deep breath and closed her eyes. "Oh yeah. I knew that." I studied her, wondering if she'd actually forgotten that I'd fired Drake and traded to the Stallions last week, or if she'd just assumed I'd still have publicity events and campaigns out of state.

"I have a new agent now too, same one as Frankie. I'm not going to be traveling much in the off-season anymore, and nothing else the rest of the summer. I'll be right here, baby. With you. Until training starts, I just have to make it to the gym to work out, and that's only a couple miles away. You can come," I offered, wanting to pounce on the opportunity to get her out of the house while she was alert and talking.

She shook her head with a sad little smile. I think she was remembering the last time we shared a workout session in Wes's basement. I hope she wasn't thinking that couldn't happen again. We'd be back to that place, when we rushed through our workouts because we couldn't keep our hands off each other. We would. Maybe not tomorrow, but someday. I had to believe it.

PEPPER

I'm going through the motions, attending doctor's appointments, changing out of pajamas into real clothes, showering, eating, speaking, but nothing is changing. Not really. I suppose it's getting easier to leave the darkness of the bedroom, if only because I'm making it part of my routine again. But the pain is still paralyzing. It doesn't allow room for any other emotions besides sadness. The therapist we're seeing, Nancy, asks questions and I answer them. We talk about how I'm feeling, how Jace is feeling, and I guess that's supposed to help, but even as I attempt to verbalize what's happening inside of me, I still don't feel like I'm really *living*. It's as if I've forgotten how.

At least I'm answering my own phone calls now, responding to emails from Finn. I'd forgotten to pull out of the Chicago half marathon, and I have to get in touch with the race directors at the last minute. Nancy, Jace, and well, everyone, tell me not to look at what the media is saying, but it's time. Almost two months have passed since we lost the baby, since the news about Monica's doping came out. She claims that it only started this year, as she was getting older and felt the pressure to keep up with the "younger generation" of distance runners. I'd always felt that instead of the leadership position she *could* have embraced, Monica was resentful that she wasn't fifteen years younger, at the beginning of her career. Rather than going with the natural flow of the Newbound team dynamics, she fought it. I don't know if the doping really did start recently or had been going on for a long while, maybe throughout her career. It's possible this is just when she finally got caught. To me, it doesn't matter, but to those women she beat unfairly and stole Olympic team spots or podium finishes from, it's devastating to wonder what could have been. If she beat them by cheating, she took away potential sponsorships, opportunities to take running careers in a new direction. One place can make a big difference depending on the race.

As I lie on the living room couch, scrolling through the articles about the scandal and the various reactions from runners, some of whom are now retired, there's a stirring in my belly. It's a buzzing, and as I let it bubble to the surface, the realization of what's happening has me sitting up all the way.

Jace turns to look at me from where he's sitting. My feet are in his lap as he's watching more football videos, analyzing players on the Stallions, his new team. "What's up, Pep?"

"I'm reading about Monica Herrick."

Jace's face hardens with concern.

"And I'm feeling something." There's excitement in my voice, and Jace's shoulders tighten as he braces himself, clearly confused about where this is going. "I'm angry. And not for myself. I'm angry on behalf of all the runners Monica beat over the years, the people she might have cheated out of money they needed to make a living running, positions on world teams in order to get those sponsorship deals, the chance to stand on an Olympic podium."

Jace puts down the remote and moves my feet off his lap. He reaches for my laptop and places it on the coffee table, leaning forward so he's lying across the couch beside me. "You sound really happy about this, though."

"Jace," I tell him, urging him to understand, "I've felt nothing but sadness and pain for almost two months. The only other feelings have been some empathy I guess for you and Gran, and that's the reason I started trying in the first place. I hated how sad and helpless I was making you feel." We'd talked about this with Nancy, acknowledged that without the bond to Jace, the love between us, the motivation to pull through this would be hard to find. But that was more from a deep love, which I guess is more like an innate part of who I am than a separate emotion.

"Anyway," I continue, "this is the first thing aside from what I feel for you that I've felt for anyone else really. The first strong feeling. It's not connected to my sadness, it's just my genuine response to what happened. I think that's a good thing, right?" My voice wavers at the question, as I recognize how ridiculous this sounds.

Jace's face breaks into a small smile. "Yeah, Pep, it's a really good thing."

My body sags in relief at his approval, his understanding that this is a big step. A breakthrough of sorts.

I expect Jace to take advantage of the moment, to put his lips on mine. After all, he's lying right beside me, the length of his body pressed against mine, our faces inches apart. And it's been weeks, six to be exact, since we've touched in any intimate way. But he doesn't do that. Instead, he asks if I want to get some fresh air and go for a walk. I'm disappointed, but I get it. He doesn't want to push. Or maybe it's only because we're at Gran's house, and our roommates could return any minute from their group grocery shopping trip. I still don't know if they normally all go run errands together, or if they're doing it to give us privacy, but in any case, I'd rather not have the four of them walk in on us.

We take Dave with us, on the same trail we've been walking on nearly every day for the past few weeks. But this time, it's not obligation that has me at Jace's side, hand in hand. I didn't have to force myself to leave the house, shield myself from the sunshine peeking through the trees, the brightness trying to shine on us. Nope, today it feels natural. The sadness is still right there, heavy in my steps, but there's a tiny bit of hope brewing too. Hope that I will be okay again, that I'll be *me*. That maybe I can start living again.

Chapter Twenty-Two

PEPPER

I read more about the scandal, and when I find commentary about my own involvement, the *feelings* really start to flow. At first, people wondered if everyone on Newbound was doping. Jace had arranged to have my blood test results made public, which I know I'd agreed to, though it was all a fog. Those results showed that everything was normal only two days after my half marathon, except, of course, that I was pregnant. Once the entire story of my pregnancy and subsequent miscarriage was revealed, it didn't eliminate all suspicion, though the general consensus was that I was clean. Some people thought it was too unbelievable that I'd run so fast, qualified for the Olympic Trials, while pregnant. I *must* have been doping, they said. Those were the same people who said that I had the miscarriage because I was doping. Surprisingly, that accusation didn't bother me. Probably because it was simply false and the opinion didn't gain any traction. Especially once it came out that I'd quit the Newbound team weeks before Monica was caught, and I hadn't known anything about it. Other women on the team, also fighting to clear their names, confirmed that I'd trained almost exclusively on my own and was rarely even in Arizona, where the doping occurred.

In the end, it all felt so out of my control. The opinions of others, I couldn't help what they said about me. It had always been that way. All I could do was tell the truth, and deal with the haters.

Most of the discussion about me had blown over after a week or two, with the general conclusion being that I hadn't been involved. I'd been a solid runner for a long time now. Sure, I was transitioning to longer distances and still early in my professional career, but I'd been steady in my growth. There was nothing unusual about my recent performances. Yes, they had been great results, but not out of the ordinary. Yes, I'd been pregnant, but the passing out afterward just went to show I was, indeed, human.

Somehow, reading all the gossip doesn't hurt as much as I expect. Not because I'm numb to it, though maybe that's part of it. No, the petty nature of it actually helps me see how unimportant it really is. People will say things about my pregnancy and the miscarriage, but they don't know shit. They don't know me.

The truth is, the intense training in the early weeks may have contributed to the miscarriage. Dr. Burch said that's highly unlikely since everything looked great right after the race, but I cling to that small chance and blame myself. It's easier than the alternative. That it just happened for no reason at all.

Nancy helped me see that at one of our sessions. She'd asked, point blank, "What if Dr. Burch told you that the miscarriage happened because you ran too hard? How would that make you feel?"

I couldn't believe it when she'd asked me that. It took me a few days to be honest with myself about the answer. The truth is, even if I had a clear reason to blame myself, I'd still have to forgive myself. I didn't even know I was pregnant, and I had no reason to suspect it, aside from a mild upset stomach a week earlier.

I've been thinking a lot about forgiveness, and realize I give it so easily to others but not myself.

"I think I'm ready to go running," I tell Jace. We're sitting on the back porch, each of us catching up on emails after breakfast. It's almost July, almost time for Jace to start training with the team again.

Jace's face lights up, and he's in his running clothes, vibrating with energy, before I have a chance to think it through. Two months. It's been two months since I've run. I haven't gone that long since I'd gotten injured in high school. And I'd at least done pool running and cross training during that time.

But it's a step toward forgiving myself. Even if it hurts and feels off, I need to let myself have this.

As soon as my feet hit pavement, it doesn't feel off at all. Nope, it's exactly right. I take a deep breath of mile-high air and smile my first genuine smile in a long time.

We run in silence, and we don't go far. Well, for me it's not far. Four miles is Jace's max, but it's just enough for me to taste what I've been missing. Finally, I'm alive again. My body is rejoicing in the gift I'm finally allowing it to have again, and strangely, I almost sense a repairing of my broken heart happening inside of me. I've finally given myself permission to start healing. I'm not just showing up to survive anymore. I actually want to be in the moment, right here with my best friend, the love between us unbreakable.

Jace leads me back a different way through the neighborhood and slows a couple blocks from Shadow Lane. He points to a rundown house on a corner lot with a sign out front.

"It's for sale."

I look at the house, note the roof is caving in, and glance at Jace. He chuckles and bites his lip. "We'd raze it and build something new. It's a great lot. Right against the foothills and around the corner from Shadow Lane." He shrugs. "I know you probably aren't ready to start thinking about it yet, but now that I'll be with the Stallions, we can get our own place."

When I throw my arms around Jace's neck, he stumbles back, unprepared for my enthusiasm. "Baby," I tell him into his neck, "I know you would do anything for me, but why don't you at least see how the commute goes during pre-season training? You might realize it's harder than you thought."

Jace lifts me up off the ground and swings me around. He's been so careful around me these past few weeks that my body responds immediately to the closeness. Jace tenses when he realizes what's happening between us, puts me back on my feet and steps backward.

"Wes wants us to check out a house by him too," Jace tells me. "If we don't want to deal with building something new, there are lots of other options. But I thought it might be a fun project. Something besides running, and... everything else, for you to enjoy."

I tilt my head as I watch him. He's been thinking a lot about this. About me. Us. Our future. I'm ready to start thinking about all these things too, but right now, I just want to be back in his arms. But my husband has thrown up an invisible wall between us. I didn't know it was possible to be so emotionally connected to someone while being so physically disconnected. The first couple years of marriage, we endured not being as physically close as we wanted because circumstances forced it. Now we have the chance to be together all the time and Jace isn't touching me.

We walk the couple of blocks home hand in hand. That's been the extent of physical touch lately. It's like we're middle schoolers dating for the first time, not a married couple. He's been patient with me, I can do the same.

"Yeah, I'm down for at least looking around. Seeing what's out there. We've never house-shopped before. It could be fun." I squeeze his hand, reassuring him that I'm back now. I'm not so fragile anymore. I'm even excited for the next adventures together.

JACE

I should have known that it would be running that brought Pepper back to me. I knew that it took therapy sessions and time to get to a point where she felt ready to run, but once she was back on the trails, the light in my girl turned back on. She'd been showing up each day, getting through it, and when one day turned into two, and two turned into weeks, then a month passed, I wondered if I'd lost her. Now, she was coming back to me, and I was so fucking relieved. And desperate not to send her back to that dark place she was at before.

Preseason training started and while I went to the stadium, Pepper met up with people to run. She'd even been doing her strength training at local gyms instead of Wes's basement. News had spread fast that we were in town to stay, and all the local fitness centers were reaching out to Pep hoping she'd make an appearance. I knew she was still hurting, but she was accepting it, trying to go after life again like she used to.

Two weeks into pre-season training, and I was finding my place on the team. No, that wasn't right – I had a place, sure, but there was tension. There was Frankie, Tanner, Calvin and others who welcomed a change in leadership, were ready to say goodbye to Troy Bremer. On the field, he was as much of an asshole as he was off of it. Every quarterback needed confidence. But Troy was arrogant. It was a wonder he'd led the team for nearly a decade with any success. From what I could tell, he'd earned his position as leader through fear. He'd bullied and belittled others into following him. Funny to think three-hundred-pound grown men could be bullied, but Troy had managed it. Taking his lead, those followers refused to show me any respect, refused to acknowledge I'd joined the team to fill Troy's shoes when he retired.

It didn't bother me. Things were already shifting. People respected that I'd dropped my agent and handled the transaction on my own. I wasn't a rookie anymore, but with only three years under my belt, there weren't many who would have made such a risky move. I didn't see it as risky, it just made sense to me, screw the fallout I'd have to deal with, but the guys thought it took balls, and that got me some approval even from Troy's crew.

I knew it would all shake out and fall into place eventually, and I didn't really give a shit about Troy's ego. I was killing it on the field, establishing a solid and steady presence. The team needed that with Troy's hot head. He'd tried throwing insults my way in an attempt to get me riled or take me down a few pegs, but I saw through him.

I loved the game, but it wasn't my life. At the end of the day, it was my job. I could tackle people for fun and play competitively, but I didn't need to be in the NFL to be complete. Troy did, and he knew he was on his way out. I almost felt bad for the dude. If I didn't have Pepper, I could've ended up like him.

She was more important to me than the shifting power dynamics on the Stallions. After practice, I'd go home to her, hear about her day, try to make her smile, talk about houses, eat some good food with crazy old people, walk Dave...

"Yo, Wilder, you listening, man?" Calvin called to me from the other side of the locker alcove.

"Nah man, ready to get home to my wife. I'm done with you fuckers." I told him the truth. I'd made it clear from day one I was a family man, not into the off-field activities Troy Bremer and his crew got up to.

Calvin laughed and shook his head. He had Leah. He knew how it was. This life was demanding. We had to get our family time when we could. "Don't I know it, man. We're goin' out tomorrow night though. First two weeks of pre-season are done. It's tradition."

Frankie walked into our alcove, towel around his waist. He jumped in. "Yeah dude, we're all going," he said with a pointed look. "The whole team doesn't get together like this much, but it's a thing. You gotta be there."

I ran a towel through my wet hair and pulled on a pair of sweats. "Yeah, I hear you. I'll be there."

Even if, or *especially because*, there was a division going on, we were still a team and had to stay a united front. Playing along in a casual setting outside of practice with everyone there, it'd be a chance to smooth over the tension off the field. But I already knew what the scene would be, based on locker room talk from Bremer and his guys. It would be like some of the parties with the Browns. An unspoken rule that no girlfriends, fiancées, or wives would be there. The only women allowed to the private team events weren't exactly hookers, but they were there for a specific purpose. Entertain, don't get attached, no strings and no expectations. Let the guys unwind with that simple understanding. It made my blood fucking boil just being in that environment.

"But I'm bringing Pepper. You guys should bring your wives too," I told Frankie, Calvin, and a few other guys in our alcove. They all turned and looked at me like I'd lost my mind. I probably had. Of all the times to bring Pepper to something like this, she wasn't in the best state of mind. But I wasn't putting up with Bremer's shit for an entire season. Especially since it wasn't clear he was planning on leaving next season without a push out the door. I hadn't bothered making a statement like this with the Browns. I knew I'd be leaving the team eventually. But the Stallions? I'd be here for the rest of my career if I could help it. Pepper and I were making this home. If it didn't work out, I didn't think I had it in me to trade and move us somewhere else. So I was doing this my way, setting the tone for how I planned to lead the team one day.

I didn't mean to bring the power shift to a head so quickly. I'd meant to let it ride out for a while, on and off the field. But after Drake, I was tired of letting shit ride. It was time to take control. And I wouldn't put up with women throwing themselves at me when I had a ring on my finger and a scowl on my face. The other guys, some just married, some with kids at home, they shouldn't have to put up with that shit either just because a dozen or so of their teammates wanted it.

I pulled a shirt over my head and looked each guy in the eye until they all gave me a nod of understanding.

Now, I just hoped Pepper was up for the challenge too.

Chapter Twenty-Three

PEPPER

I'm prepared for tonight to be excruciating. If I'd had a hard time at Frankie's wedding, I have to assume a night at a club in Denver with the Stallions will be rough. Jace has been firmly at my side, supporting me, and I'm going to do the same. I dress for the night like I'm preparing for battle. I head over to Zoe's, and tell her the occasion. With the exception of Frankie's wedding, this is our first time out in months. I want to look stunning, not just to get in the right mental state for the evening, but for Jace.

Zoe dresses me in a shiny gold bandage dress of hers with matching heels. She does something to my hair to make it so wavy it's almost curly. I'd normally be embarrassed in an outfit like this, but with half the wives in attendance current or former supermodels, I know I won't stand out.

Jace just shakes his head when I tell him this. We stand outside his Jeep, both with our hands on our hips. "You can't seriously think you're going to blend in wearing that."

"Jace, we're going to a club called Red Hot. How do you think other women will be dressed there?"

Jace shuts his eyes like he's in pain. "Pep, I told you, it's going to be tense as shit when the wives and girlfriends show up. I need to be on my game. There's no way in hell I'm going to be thinking about anything but you." His voice rises as he works himself up but then stops himself before continuing, gesturing wildly in my direction.

"But me, what?" I take a step closer.

Jace opens his mouth and closes it a few times before letting his head drop in defeat. He opens the passenger side door for me and I sigh as I attempt to get in without splitting the dress in two. Jace averts his eyes even though I'm sure I'm flashing him. He's been trying so hard to be a gentleman, and I don't understand it. Is he afraid I'll get pregnant again? I went back on birth control weeks ago. It wasn't an easy decision but I wasn't even close to being ready to have another baby.

I don't want to mention his lack of affection toward me lately. Yes, he's been incredibly attentive and sweet but he doesn't even cuddle me at night. I want to be fair and show him the same patience he showed me, but I'm struggling.

When we finally pull up to the valet in front of the club, cameras flash as we get out of Jace's twenty-year-old Jeep. I love that he still drives this thing. We go up a flight of stairs before entering the dark club. Troy Bremer and a few other players I recognize storm over as soon as they spot us. I notice the flock of women they leave in their wake. Jace warned me what to expect, and I straighten my spine before putting on my best sweet and innocent smile.

"Hi guys!" I wave enthusiastically while Jace wraps a protective arm around my waist.

"Pepper." Troy nods at me. "I think your husband was mistaken. Tonight is players only."

I feign confusion as I glance behind him and the two other guys crowding us. "Who are they? Were the cheerleaders invited?"

One of the guys next to Troy smirks and the other coughs to hide his laughter. "No. They're here to help us unwind." Troy's tone even *sounds* sleazy as he makes the confession.

My eyes widen at Troy's audacity, and this time I'm not even faking it. I thought he'd make some excuse. I wasn't expecting him to be so direct.

"I don't know if you're aware of this," Jace says slowly. "But my wife just lost a baby." His voice is low, and it sends a chill down my spine. "You will not insult her, or our marriage, by insinuating that all the players on this team unwind in the same way you do."

I sense a presence behind us, and Frankie's voice booms. "Lizzie's here to help me unwind. Even if it means she's gotta endure my dance moves."

Lizzie laughs. "Has anyone ever told you your hand-eye coordination sucks, Mr. Defensive Lineman?"

"Dancing is not about hand eye-coordination, sweetheart," Frankie rebuts. "It's not my fault I've got too much muscle to be graceful."

As the two bicker behind us, more couples arrive.

Troy isn't prepared to back down, but the guys next to him shrug. One of them punches the other on the shoulder. "More single ladies for us then." And they return to the waiting women by the bar. Troy is fuming when we step around him to find our own spot at the bar.

It's an amazing night. I'm not training hard, I'm not pregnant, and I've got a little victory to celebrate on Jace's behalf, so I drink. And dance. And sing. I've got a new group of women I can start calling friends, and even better? Their men are linked to Jace's world, which means we can all hang out together, share the same experiences.

Jace isn't drinking since he's driving us home, so I'm surprised when he lets down his guard and presses my body into his as we dance. His lips drop to my neck, and I feel him throbbing, hot and hard at my backside. It's been so long since I've had this connection with him, that for a moment I wonder if he's just staking a claim, making a point. But with half the team with significant others, and the other half enjoying the, uh, single ladies, no one's paying attention to us.

I turn in his arms and ask if we can get out of here. He nods, eyes smoldering into mine even as his jaw clenches, the telltale sign all is not right in Jace Wilder World.

Jace guides me outside, and I lean into him for support. Between the three cocktails I had at the club and these heels, I need his sturdy frame. I'm tipsy, for maybe the first time in years, but I try to hide it as we wait for the valet to bring our car around. Who knows if there's press around waiting for an embarrassing photo op. My arms wrap around Jace's strong body and I hum into his broad chest. I really want to crawl up his body, but this will have to do.

Jace drives a bit aggressively through the city, and I place my hand on his thigh, partly in an attempt to calm him, but mostly to maintain that physical connection to him. I sense him closing down, trying to put distance between us. He doesn't mention a detour to a campground, and given the determined expression on his profile, I'm guessing he's planning to use the drive home to cool off.

I shouldn't be pissed. After all, I was in my own world, barely communicating, for weeks. But as I bring my hand back to my own lap and Jace turns up the radio, I find my fists clenching. We've been so good at communicating. Jace has come so far. But this? We don't know how to talk about it. I can't even talk to my friends about what's going on. It's too personal. And I'm afraid to raise it with Jace. What if it comes out like I'm questioning his manhood? Isn't that, like, the number one thing to never do in a marriage?

Maybe if I phrase it differently... "Jace?" My voice comes out small, and at first I'm not sure he's heard me over the music.

He turns it down and flicks his gaze over to mine. "Yeah, Pep?"

A lump lodges in my throat when I start to ask him if he's still attracted to me. I realize it's a dumb question the moment the words start to form. I felt him against me at the club. I can feel the want coming off him in waves right now as easily as I can feel it in my own body.

Instead, I ask the question I'm even more terrified to ask. "Why won't you touch me?" My voice is hoarse, and I have to force it out of my mouth over the resistance in my throat.

His grip on the wheel tightens and I realize this was a bad place to raise such a difficult topic.

"I touch you," he says, but only halfheartedly. He knows what I'm asking.

"No, you don't. I haven't pushed it because I got the feeling you wanted the space, and I want to respect that. But, this isn't something I want to talk about in front of Nancy. And I don't understand it. Are you worried I'll get pregnant again?" I hold my breath waiting for his answer. I've assumed we'll try again, but we haven't discussed when. What if he doesn't want kids anymore?

"No." Jace doesn't hesitate with his answer. It's sharp and strong, but it also suggests he's not going to say more.

"Jace, I need you to talk to me. Or touch me. *Now*."

We're on the highway, halfway between Denver and Brockton. Touching would be tricky, so he better start talking.

"Pep, you haven't been yourself for a while. I know you're doing awesome, baby. Tonight was amazing. But I don't want to push you back to that place. There's no rush."

"Jace, the boner you have right now just talking about this tells me there is, in fact, a rush."

I'm not trying to be funny. Okay, maybe I am a little, but Jace laughs harder than I expect. So hard, a tear trickles out the corner of his eye.

"I've been trying my best to hide it, Pep," he says when he catches his breath. "But I'm practically always in this state around you these days. And tonight did not fucking help." He shifts in his seat, attempting to ease the obvious strain in his pants.

I throw my hands up. "Stop trying to hide it. Jace, we're married! I'm so turned on right now I want to start touching myself. What are we doing?"

Jace throws his head back and groans. "Don't say that, Pep."

I squeeze my legs together and mutter, "It's true."

"What if you're not ready?"

I let out a huff that almost sounds like a growl. Last time Jace thought I "wasn't ready" for him, I ended up dating Ryan Harding and Jace spiraled out of control with his delinquent activities. I'm tempted to remind him but we're both on edge. The edge is entirely sexual, but still.

"I'm ready," I tell him. "*Please*." Great, I've resorted to begging my husband for sex.

There's silence for a moment and when Marvin Gaye starts singing "Let's get it on," from the radio we both start laughing hysterically. "You've gotta be fucking kidding me." Jace's amusement is mixed with obvious frustration. He puts on a different station.

Jace finally pulls off the highway at the Brockton exit and makes his way toward Shadow Lane. He pulls into his dad's driveway, and I'm surprised when he guides us toward Jim's house.

"Jim's out at his new girlfriend's place tonight. We've got it to ourselves."

Jace doesn't look at me when he says this, but my libido immediately perks up at what this might mean. As soon as we're inside, Jace doesn't even bother to turn on the lights before caging my body against the door.

"Pepper, I started something only once since we lost the baby," he says, his voice gentle. Nancy has encouraged us to just say those words, don't avoid them. "And you wouldn't let me touch you. You got me off, but then you curled into yourself. I heard you crying afterward, baby, and it crushed me. And then you disappeared into yourself for weeks. You know I want you. But I don't want you enough to lose you to that darkness."

I touch his cheek. "Jace, me hurting had nothing to do with what happened that night. I had no idea you thought that. All I wanted was to give you something, knowing you were hurting too. But I cried because I didn't want to let myself feel so much. We talked about this in therapy. I wasn't letting myself enjoy anything because I was blaming myself. Letting all those emotions in would rip me open too wide."

Jace's eyes search mine, and I can see that he's scared to rip me open again. And that he's blaming himself for the depression I sunk into.

"You don't know that though," Jace says. "Maybe going down on me like you did was too much. Maybe if I touch you now it will be too much, again, and you'll stop running again, stop living, and fuck, baby, I can't see you go back to that place again."

I place a hand on his chest, trying to calm him.

"Jace, I gave you a blow job because I love you and your hard-on looked painful. I loved giving you that and it did not cause me to sink into depression." I'm going for a matter-of-fact tone that will convince him, but with all the ups and downs from the night, my explanation makes Jace laugh again.

He shakes his head. "Please don't say blow job right now or I'll come in my pants like I did that first time we made out."

And then we're both laughing.

"You know what?" I ask. "You thinking you caused me to sink into depression even though it's not true, maybe it's a little like how I'm feeling about losing the baby. I can't prove that the race didn't cause it, but I'm convinced I'm guilty anyway. Just like you can't prove that intimacy a week after the miscarriage is the reason I didn't come out of the house for a week." Jace's eyes bore into mine as I speak. "You think maybe you're just looking to control something? You need to feel that guilt to feel control?" It's a harsh question, but we've talked so much about, well, everything else, over the years and especially with Nancy the past few weeks, it doesn't seem so out of the blue.

Jace tilts his head to the side and before I know it, he's stripping. Right there in his dad's foyer.

"Come on baby, let's go downstairs." I mean, I'm all for the strip tease, but it's still weird standing by the front door to Jim's house.

But Jace stops when he has his shirt off. There's a tattoo on his chest. It's tiny, and I have to lean closer to see it. Wings, with the inscription, *Baby Wilder*, and the date of my miscarriage.

"I got it a couple of days ago."

A couple of days ago? Man, he was either making a point to keep it from me or it has been way too long since I've seen this man naked. He sleeps shirtless beside me each night but I guess the last couple of nights he slipped under the covers before I got a good look.

My fingers trace the tattoo and I kiss it. "I love it."

Jace takes my hand. "Maybe it's time we start forgiving ourselves for shit out of our control. Baby Wilder's always going to be in our hearts, ya know? Just because we aren't hanging on to guilt or some other shitty emotion doesn't mean we're forgetting him."

I smile through the tears streaming down my cheeks. So I wasn't being crazy with my questions. "We need to let ourselves be happy. No more holding on to guilt, trying to blame ourselves for shit out of our control," I agree with a sniffle.

Jace's lips crash to mine. They stay locked on mine as he scoops me up and jogs down the stairs to his old bedroom, where I had my very first orgasm. And he gives me many, many more throughout the night.

Chapter Twenty-Four

PEPPER

Coach Harding has been reaching out to check in, making it clear that whenever I'm ready, he's there to sit down and talk business. The meeting is long overdue. I meet Coach Harding and Ryan at a coffee shop in town a couple of days after the club and subsequent late night – early morning – basically all-nighter in Jace's old room. I'm still riding the high from having my husband back completely, from making the joint decision that letting go of guilt and anger doesn't mean letting go of Baby Wilder.

"You've been back running with Lexi and Sienna, even joined them in a few of their shorter workouts. We'd love to have you join the group in a more official capacity," Coach Harding tells me.

Ryan slides forward. "We're going to expand the group a bit, and we've been talking with other runners – women and men, who are training for the marathon. Remember Indigo Adams? She won the Atlanta half."

"Oh yeah. She's got a serious kick." I followed her for several miles so could probably pick out the back of her head in a line-up, but I'm not actually sure what her face looks like.

"She trains solo right now, doesn't even have a coach," Ryan says, not hiding his respect for this runner. "I think she'll make the move here if she knows she'll have others her pace to push her. Like you, she's never run a marathon. Her first will be at the trials in February. That's a little over six months from now," Ryan adds, as if I can't do math.

Mark asks the question looming in the air. "Before we make any representations to Indigo or the other female runners considering joining the group, we want to ask where your head's at. Are you looking to train for the marathon trials in six months? It's completely up to you, Pepper. If you want to wait and tackle a different goal or simply see how things go, the ball's in your court."

This is the kind of coaching I need. I need people who actually care about what they saw me go through this summer, who understand that the loss I suffered isn't an isolated experience. It affected my entire life, not only my running fitness, but my outlook on racing and competing in general. Three days ago I might have taken Coach Harding up on his willingness to see how it goes, not make any hard commitment to a particular race or training plan. But I'm done with guilt. I deserve to go after my goals.

"I'm all in. I think we should make this group more official too. Maybe give it a team name? I know you've been coaching your former college runners informally for a while," I tell Mark, "but with Ryan now filling in when you're too busy with the college team, I like the direction you're going. Building up the numbers on the team, having coaching contracts."

I can tell Mark and Ryan weren't expecting this response from me, but they don't hesitate to dive into discussions about which runners would be a good addition, trying to get some sponsorships behind the team as a whole rather than individual runners. I'm grateful to be able to use my name – which I know simply has more power as Jace's wife – toward a greater purpose than my own running. This is what was missing from my running career – a team. And with Ryan and Mark brainstorming beside me, I feel like I could be an integral part of it, not just for my running accolades, but in leadership too.

Within weeks, we've got three new women runners in addition to me, Lexi and Sienna, and three new guy runners to join Brax, Ryan and the others. Brax found a house a little ways up in the foothills with enough bedrooms for almost everyone to stay. It's nothing fancy, but a step up from the rundown place they'd been staying at the past couple of years since graduating college. With the exception of Maisy White, one of our new runners, no one else on the team is married. Since there isn't quite enough space for all of us in the running house, it's easy for Maisy and me to opt out. I'm ready not to have roommates, no matter how much I love Gran or my teammates.

We meet up at the running house one night to decide on a team name. We're all on board that we don't want to pick a team name that's tied to a main sponsor, like Newbound. That way we have more independence in choosing sponsors. I propose the Brockton Babes, but the guys veto that immediately. Sienna tells them they can be the Brockton Bros if they want something more manly, but we end up deciding the same name for both genders is best. Lexi pushes for Brockton Badasses, but Ryan reminds us a lot of race directors and sponsors will give us a hard time with that one. We finally decide on the Brockton Beasts. There is no dispute that the team will remain Brockton-based, and while we consider throwing the Harding name in there somehow, Ryan and Mark don't want that. Even in choosing the team name it's a democratic effort, and I like the precedent it sets for the dynamic going forward.

That burn in my belly is back, the one people call competitive drive. I think it was just waiting to be lit, and it took a number of puzzle pieces refitting themselves back together to get it going again. Indigo Adams, who goes by Indy, is the youngest on the team – she's only a year out of college. Kendra Smith is my age – we used to race each other in high school, and she just qualified for the trials at the half at Chicago. She'd been training in Oregon, where she went to college, but after breaking up with her boyfriend out there, she was hoping to come back to Colorado. Maisy White is the oldest in the group, and the only one who's run a marathon before. She was a senior at UC when Sienna was a freshman.

All of the new runners are just as competitive and driven as the rest of us, but unlike the Newbound team, there aren't any big egos in the group. When we recruited runners, we looked for women one of us knew personally or at least had reputations for being drama-free and relatively humble.

We're doing a short training block for a tune-up half marathon in early October, and then we'll start the intense training for the trials, which will be held in Houston in February. Lexi and Sienna haven't yet qualified for the trials, and they're hoping to hit their times in October. Of course, technically we'll be competing against one another for the three spots on the Olympic team, but training together should make all of us better, give us all a better shot than if we were training alone. At the end of the day, making the Olympic team is a long shot for any one of us. It all comes down to one race, one day, and anything can happen in a marathon.

My new routine is waking up with Jace, then breakfast with Gran and the crew before Jace heads off to practice and I go to meet the girls for a run. Then I usually take a quick break for more food before going to one of the fitness centers in town for strength training and stretches. Sometimes I have a second afternoon run, but only a couple times a week. Once a week I get a massage to keep the muscles from getting too tight. Jace usually returns mid-afternoon and we hang out, sometimes meet friends for dinner or go out to a restaurant. We're still seeing Nancy every other week too. At night, Jace watches football or studies football on his computer while I do my emails and sponsorship stuff and we go to bed early. Some might find our simple life boring. There's no glamour, no fast cars, and we haven't had a big night out since Red Hot. The black-tie fundraisers for the players peter off once the season starts, and we don't seek out opportunities to be in the spotlight.

It's exactly the life I want. Some days are hard. Some days I think about what I would be doing right now if I was still pregnant. Some days I go back to feeling guilty for loving to run, wonder if I deserve the happiness it brings me, the hope and excitement I feel about a hard workout, the next race, chasing that win. Sometimes, I have to work hard just to get out of bed and face the day and let it bring me joy.

But Jace is doing it by my side, and that makes it easier.

"What do you think?" Jace asks.

We're standing on a balcony to a master bedroom. The house is half a mile up the road from Wes and Zoe, and the view is jaw-dropping.

"It's too big," I say on a sigh. "I know the idea is to grow into it someday. I know that it will be great to have space to host runners training, friends visiting, whatever, but..." I lean into his side. "It's not us."

Jace puts his hand around my waist and pulls me close. "I could dig this view every morning, but we can hit up Wes and Zoe for a view. And we walk up the trail to a view like this almost every afternoon anyway. The house doesn't feel like a home, does it?"

"No. I know it's staged right now or whatever and we'll make it more personal if it's ours, but it's too... nice? It's not even ostentatious or showy really, it's just so far from the cozy homes we grew up in, that's not how I see us, or who I want us to be."

"Or how I see our kids growing up," Jace adds.

We've talked about kids a little more openly. I want to try again. Maybe as soon as after the trials if I don't make the Olympics.

"This kind of house makes sense for Zoe and Wes. I'm not saying it's wrong for everyone. Zoe likes shiny things, not in a bad way, but she's loving the pool, throwing parties, stuff like that. And Wes grew up in a place like this."

"Let's build our own place. We can make it our own. Just the way we want it."

"Plus, that lot is on Pleasant Way. That has to mean it's got good vibes."

Jace's chest vibrates in laughter. "Pleasant Way," he says with a shake of his head. "Now if we just paint the house pink I'll complete my image as the NFL's wholesome family man."

"Nah, you've got a tattoo now. You're still a badass, babe, don't worry."

"As long as my wife still thinks I'm a badass," he says, nuzzling my neck.

"I'd be down with more tattoos," I admit.

"I'll get one for each baby we make," he promises with a whisper in my ear.

A throat clears behind us. "Mr. and Mrs. Wilder?" Jane, our realtor, asks.

Oh, right, we're touring a house with our realtor. I'd nearly forgotten.

"We're going to make an offer on the Pleasant Way lot," Jace informs her. I love his decisiveness.

She looks a little disappointed. I'm sure the commission on this one would have made her day. Or year. But she doesn't push. Jace can be so sweet to me I often forget how intimidating other people find him.

As we go back downstairs and through the house, we talk about plans for razing the place falling apart on Pleasant Way and building a new house. I think about how excited Gran and Lulu will be to help with the project. "I'm not really into pink, but how do you feel about a polka-dotted house?" I ask Jace. "I mean, if Gran's going to be involved, we'll have to make some concessions."

"We can paint one interior room however she wants. And maybe a door. But I get veto power over any exterior painting decisions."

That's fair. But purple is my favorite color and I'd really dig coming home to a purple house. Maybe I can at least talk him into painting the front door purple. Oh, this is going to be fun.

"Hey, I know it's last minute. But I want to come to your first game with the Stallions this weekend. Should I talk to Denise about travel arrangements?" Denise is Jace's new PA. Jace's PA before was Drake's assistant, and I avoided talking to both of them. Denise, on the other hand, is so sweet I find myself looking for chances to call her about random things.

"You sure? I'd love that, Pep, but you've got that half next month and I know how important it is to rest during this training block."

I give Jace a look that says, *I love you but stop it.* Yes, training and resting appropriately is my job but it's only a piece of my life; Jace is a bigger piece. I know that he's not meant to play in this game, and may not even play in games all season, but I also know how much it means to *me* when I have him nearby, supporting me, no matter how big or small each step is. I want to give that back to him. And I also know he's on his way to leading this team. I want everyone to see us as a united front, even if I do have my own athletic goals that will keep me away sometimes.

"I'd love that, but I can arrange everything with Denise," he relents, kissing the tip of my nose.

"No way. Denise is my bud. I'll call her."

Man, it's nice to know good people are on our teams, finally.

We ask Jane to drop us at Wes and Zoe's place. It's time to finish the puzzle we started months ago, still sitting half complete on their dining room table.

Chapter Twenty-Five

PEPPER

I don't know that there's ever been as much attention on me for a race as there is for this one. It's a big half marathon, a stacked international race with lots of Olympic team contenders trying to set the tone for the trials, make their place known. With all the media attention throughout the summer about Newbound, Monica, Ray, there was bound to be increased interest in my performance. But add in the miscarriage, me changing teams and coaches even before the scandal broke, and my so-called "comeback" after a couple months completely off from training, and I've unintentionally gained a spotlight position on the start line.

It doesn't make me uncomfortable. Not anymore. It's not only that I've gotten used to being in the spotlight as Jace Wilder's wife both on and off the starting line, but too much has happened to allow me to dwell on the opinions of others. There will be people who support me, and there will always be those who criticize, no matter what happens in this race today. I've experienced a pain and loss so deep that the haters can't touch it. And I've come out of it. So today, I'll let myself go for it, and see what happens.

All five of my training partners are here today. For Sienna and Lexi, they are racing to hit the qualifying time. The half marathon qualifying time is actually a much more competitive time than the full marathon qualifying time. For a while, there was some debate about whether runners should even be able to qualify for the full by running a half. But cutting out that chance would weed out some fast runners with potential who just didn't have an opportunity to race a full for injury reasons or, in my case, because I'm new to longer distances and haven't built up to the full distance yet.

For me, Indy, Kendra, and Maisy, today is a check-in on our training. We did a short taper and we're here to get one more solid race experience under our belts, test where we're at and how training is going, before putting our heads down for the hardest training session of our lives leading up to the trials.

When the gun goes off, the six of us stick together in the back of the lead pack. The temperature is perfect brisk fall weather, but there's a solid headwind. Our training group sticks together in the back of a large lead pack. We spend the first few miles letting others break the wind, but no one wants to take the lead today with a strong headwind, and for that reason, the pace is too slow.

I glance at Indy, who seems to know what I'm thinking. We need to pick it up if we want Sienna and Lexi to get those qualifying times. We move around the group, immediately having to dig deeper in order to go against the wind.

Though we've done training runs at altitude at 5:30 pace, it doesn't feel like that smooth, solid pace we've been drilling into our systems, that I churned out with ease while pregnant. Nope. Even with the advantage of being at sea level, the headwind forces us to work for the steady pace. I almost never look behind me during a race, but my mindset for today has changed. I'm not racing for myself. Otherwise I'd sit in the back of the pack, leading as little as possible to conserve energy until the end. Today, I'm pacing for my teammates. I've already got my qualifying time. Some might think I've still got something to prove, after all that went down professionally and personally this summer. But, well, I don't give a shit.

I glance behind me and find Kendra and Maisy right on our heels, providing even more protection from the wind for Lexi and Sienna. Lexi flashes me a bright smile, telling me she's grateful for the move we've made. The pack has tagged on to our group, taking advantage of the hard work Indy and I are putting in, but I get it. They're racing smart. But they're racing for themselves. It's been years since I've had a chance to fight for something other than myself at a race. I missed being part of a real team. We might have our own agents, our own headaches with sponsors and making this work as a career, but we train hard together and we all want each other to succeed.

Jace is meant to play for the Stallions for the first time in a home game tomorrow and though I know, from my pal Denise, that he tried to figure out a way to fly in and out for this race, it was too risky. He couldn't take the chance of a flight being canceled on the way back, and he can't miss a practice or team meetings before game day. I know he's thinking of me though, and it's not so lonely. I guess I didn't even realize how lonely I'd been racing all over the country until now, when I've finally got not only one girl at my side, on my team, but four more right behind me.

Kendra and Maisy move around us at mile seven, taking over the pace. I'm grateful for the break, but I'm still feeling strong. When Kendra starts to slow at mile nine, dropping back, I take over again next to Maisy. Indy is right there with me, and with our other three teammates behind us, we charge forward. I don't know what's happening with the rest of the pack at this point, but I'm starting to pick up the pace. My teammates go with me, so I keep pushing. We've been holding steady right at the pace for the qualifying time, but as the crowds pick up and we near the final couple of miles, it's time to see what's left in our legs.

I can hear sharp breathing behind me, and I know that everyone is hurting. But we've now dug deep dozens of times together on the roads in Brockton, and when I crank it up another notch with a mile to go, I'm not alone. At the end of races, when everything burns, your legs are rubber, your lungs are bursting, it's easy to want to back off and tell yourself there's nothing left to give, to just hold on and get through the end without digging any deeper. But when the same girls who train on the same roads, do the same workouts, are pushing right there beside you, it's easier to shut off the doubts and simply go with them.

Knowing this, I don't relent on the pace even as I sense my teammates struggling around me.

When we hit mile marker twelve, my own body starts to give out from breaking the wind for nearly the entire race. Lexi overtakes me first, and my heart soars for her. She's going to hit the qualifying mark. A moment later, others who have been taking advantage of our pacing start to pass. International runners mostly, from what I can see, who are here for the prize money, not the Olympic Trials mark.

With half a mile to go, I'm hoping Sienna is still in the mix. I haven't seen my other teammates, and I'm guessing Kendra, Maisy and Indy are toast from leading just like I am. When I sense someone at my shoulder I glance over to find Sienna there, face red, arms pumping. I match her stride, and together we bring it home. I can't exactly call it a sprint to the finish, we're too spent to pick up our turnover much, but we don't ease up. And it's a good thirty seconds under the qualifying time.

All six of us are going to be in Houston for the trials. My gut clenches for a moment, recalling the last time I went through a finish line, when I didn't know I was carrying Baby Wilder. But even with the sadness sitting on my heart, I'm happy. Lexi and Sienna throw their arms around me, and I can hardly wait for the next three months of brutal training with these women.

––––––––––

I'm floating on that post-race high when I show up for Jace's game the next day. It's my third time watching a Stallions home game this season, but it will be the first time Jace is on the field. Zoe and Wes picked me up from the airport and we drove straight to the stadium. The three of us make our way up to one of the boxes reserved for players' friends and family. We had the option of sitting in regular seats, but I don't want to deal with the attention we're bound to draw from others in the stands, not to mention reporters. I'd tried that at one of the games and even without Jace playing, it was a lot.

As soon as I see who is in the box, I wish we'd taken the other seats. I'm expecting Stephanie Bremer. The past few times we've seen each other since Frankie's wedding we simply keep our distance. I'm not going to apologize for Gran's behavior, and it's not like she's about to apologize for telling me I caused the miscarriage by running too much.

"Why the hell is Madeline Brescoll here with Bremer's wife?" Wes doesn't even try to keep his question quiet. A few heads swing our way, then dart over to Madeline and Stephanie, where Wes's glare is directed.

"You have got to be kidding me," Zoe mutters.

There's only one explanation for this. "Drake Vogel."

Zoe and Wes turn to me. "Huh? Jace's old agent is here?" Wes turns to look around the stands.

"No. Drake knows Madeline from New York. He also knows she and Jace have a history."

Wes starts to nod slowly as he processes what I'm saying. "He got Bremer's wife to invite Madeline," Wes says.

Zoe tugs her bottom lip. "You know, Madeline goes back and forth between New York and Denver. She doesn't spend much time in Brockton, too small-town now for her, but it makes sense Drake would set them up. Two evil socialites."

I snicker, remembering Zoe's nickname for Madeline back in high school. "Mad-evil."

Zoe raises one eyebrow. "And Sour-efanie."

Leah's voice pipes in from beside me, "Sinfullnie has a nice ring to it too."

I hadn't noticed Angel and Leah joining the conversation.

You know, you grow up, leave the drama of high school, the stalkers from college, and yet, the mean girls just never quite grow up. They're a little sharper, a little more jaded, but still stuck in their own bitterness. In Sour-efanie's case, probably busy raising the next genera-tion of mean girls. Setting an excellent example for her daughters, I'm sure.

Sighing, I walk toward the window overlooking the field. I'm not going to miss out on the game because Drake's trying to stir up trouble by inviting Madeline. Hopefully Troy doesn't know about this and didn't try to mess with Jace's head today by saying something. I'm just hopeful that Troy's loyalty to the team is stronger than his need to prove he's still the leader.

I'm not planning on engaging, but Wes can't help himself.

"Madeline, what are you doing here?"

I take in Madeline's stance, trying to grasp whether she knew what she was getting into when she came here or if she was in the dark. When she smirks, I give myself an internal head slap. Of *course* she knew what she was doing.

"Steph invited me."

"Right," Wes replies with sarcasm. "Drake Vogel must be pretty fucking desperate if he's dragging old hookups in to try to get back at Jace for dropping him."

Madeline narrows her eyes and I'm tempted to smack Wes on the back of the head for even bothering with this little shitshow. Sure, it'll feel good to take them down a few pegs but my MO is usually to ignore and pretend they don't bother me. Seems to be just as effective in most cases, but too late for that.

"Drake's far from desperate," Madeline says with her haughty little attitude. She's still stunning, unfortunately. "He's taken on the starting quarterback for the Stallions as a new client."

My eyes widen at that news. Why would Drake take on a veteran on his way out? When Jace signed with Drake, his whole spiel was that he was all about the next generation, the newbies, that he was young, a go-getter early in his career but would be with them for years to come. Wes doesn't seem affected by this revelation, or at least he's a good faker.

He scoffs. "Then Bremer must be desperate too."

Now Stephanie steps forward, and seeing these vindictive women side by side doesn't send a shiver down my spine like it might have once upon a time. Nope, I'm struggling not to laugh at the whole situation. While it's entertaining, I sort of want it to be over so I don't miss anything. The game's about to start.

"My husband is *not* desperate. Who are *you* anyway?" Stephanie gives Wes a once-over but she's a terrible actress. She knows exactly who he is. If she's the Denver socialite she's trying to be, there's no way she wouldn't recognize Wes, the son of a famous Hollywood movie director who happened to have grown up near Denver, and who also garnered independent celebrity status in the technology industry, earning a small fortune in his own right.

Wes ignores the question. "Let me guess. Bremer dropped his agent when he pushed retirement as the smartest option? Decided to go with someone like Drake who would feed his ego and tell him he could hold on for a few more years?" Wes shakes his head. "That's just sad, man. Wilder's already a better QB than Bremer and everyone knows it. I'm getting a beer, want anything, babe?" he asks Zoe.

"I'll take a beer. Pep?"

"I'm good. But I need to get some snacks before the game starts."

I'm done with this banter, hungry, and ready to watch my husband prove Wes right.

Chapter Twenty-Six

PEPPER

Jace doesn't disappoint. I'm no football fanatic, but I do know that Jace was only meant to play in the first quarter, and is doing so well they keep him in for the second quarter too. Stephanie and Madeline sit off to the side, isolated from the rest of the players' friends and families. I feel bad for them. Okay, I don't feel bad for Madeline, but I'm a little sad for Stephanie. Her husband's an asshole. I'd heard about it, but also witnessed it first hand at Red Hot. While I was mostly in my own little happy bubble, I did catch sight of her husband groping other women. It makes my stomach churn in disgust, but she doesn't need to turn her bitterness around on me. They leave after the first half.

At least, I think they've left. When I head to the restrooms reserved for the boxed seating, they're at the counter, reapplying makeup. I default to ignore mode, do my business, and contemplate forgoing washing my hands when I find them both eyeing me in the mirror. Nah, that would make them think they won somehow. As expected, they play mean girls with me. Actually, it's mean *women* now, they've graduated to the next level. Only, this isn't like when Madeline poured her drink down my dress outside the bathroom at Remy

Laroche's party in high school. I'm no longer insecure about where I belong and who I belong with.

Stephanie starts in with a hard hit. "I hope you're not still doping to try to run fast, Pepper. Cheaters never win, so they say."

"They also have a hard time having babies," Madeline adds.

My blood boils at that comment, but as I attempt to mimic Wes's unaffected look, I remember what I was feeling just moments earlier. Pity. They're trying to get a rise out of me. Looking for a reaction. They desperately want to know that they can shake me, hurt me. And why? Because if they can, they've still got power.

So, as much as I'd love to pull a Gran and slap them across their cheeks, I settle for an eyeroll. They can't touch me. I won't let them. I take my time drying my hands, pushing down all the insults threatening to burst from my lips. Nope. I'm better than that. By saying nothing, I'm saying everything.

I've got a whole crew of friends and family willing to stick up for me, my integrity, and my marriage. If it means harsh words, a bitch slap, or a drink splashed in a face, I'm covered. The women in front of me probably don't even have each other's backs, not that I'm going to test it.

And when I walk right on out of there with nothing but a little sigh of annoyance, I can almost feel the frustration vibrating off of them. I didn't give them the satisfaction of engaging. And that's killing them.

When Jace starts again in the second half and Troy remains on the sidelines, pouting like a four- year-old, Madeline and Stephanie do leave the box. And they don't return.

After the game, I head to the hallway outside the locker room with Angel and Leah to wait for Jace. Zoe and Wes are getting a table at a restaurant so we can celebrate Jace's first full game in the NFL. He's never played an entire game, and they won by two touchdowns, so from what I understand, it's a major success.

I'm proud of him, relieved that things are going so well in his transition to the new team, despite Troy Bremer being a jackass. It's been two days since I've seen my husband though, the longest we've gone apart in months, and I miss him like crazy. Despite vibrating with the anticipation of his strong arms wrapping around me, I'm feeling incredibly thankful that two days now seems like a long time apart. A year ago, hell, even six months ago, a couple days without seeing each other would have been just a regular part of our lives.

The reporters on the other end of the hallway swarm the first couple of players as they exit the locker room. I recognize Troy Bremer immediately. He's usually one of the last to come out, probably because he likes making people wait on him. Instead of flashing his cocky smile and reveling in the attention, he scowls at the reporters and rushes past them. He doesn't bother to look to see if his wife or anyone is waiting on him, and I guess no one is.

I knew when I married Jace that there'd always be men trying to knock him down, fighting for the power and leadership that come so easily to my husband. I guess I just assumed that grown men would do it with a bit more maturity, or even subtlety. But it's clear some men and women alike are just larger versions of toddlers throwing temper tantrums.

With Troy and his posse storming by, the reporters turn in our direction. They usually stay in position by the door to try to be the first to get interviews with the players, but a couple walk our way. I glance at Angel and Leah, looking for answers, but they appear just as baffled as me.

One of the reporters, a woman not much older than me, stops in front of us.

"Pepper, there's been nearly as much fanfare about you today as there has been about your husband. How does it feel to have your name cleared?"

I stare at her in confusion. "My name was cleared? I didn't know it needed to be cleared from anything." I guess there will always be a little speculation simply from being on the same team as Monica Herrick, but I've accepted that.

The reporter raises her eyebrows. "Didn't you see the article in the Times this morning?" When I continue starting at her in confusion, she offers a smile. "Ah, I bet you traveled in this morning from your race yesterday and came straight to the game. Another indication the Wilder loyalty runs deep."

"Times article?"

She puts down her mic, and the other reporter who came over here with her heads back to the exit as another athlete comes out.

"Yes. You led your team in a headwind through a half marathon yesterday. Sacrificed your own race so that your teammates could qualify for the Olympic Trials. A cheater wouldn't demonstrate that kind of selflessness. That's the general consensus. Your teammates confirmed that this wasn't discussed before the race, you just made the decision on your own."

"Oh. Um. That's great." I'm so awkward with reporters. Especially when I'm caught off guard like this. Seriously, what am I supposed to say? She's not even asking me questions. I guess she tried to but I'm so clueless I don't even know what she's talking about.

"Well, congratulations. Stallions fans will want to celebrate your accomplishments too now that your husband is their new hero. It seems the Wilders come as a package and your fan base is about to grow exponentially." She winks before turning and going back down the hallway.

Angel and Leah laugh at my stunned expression, patting me on the back.

"Watch out," Angel tells me. "Football fans are probably a little more aggressive than the running crowd you're used to."

I really can't imagine football fans taking much interest in running, but it's sweet to think I might have even more people supporting me than I thought. I was happy with just my friends and family, but if a stadium full of people wants to stand up for my integrity as a runner and Jace's wife or whatever, I'm down.

"They don't usually serve hot dogs or beer at marathons," I point out.

Angel and Leah laugh some more. "Maybe they'll need to start," Leah says.

When Jace finally comes out of the locker room, his eyes immediately start searching for me. It reminds me of when he finished his games in college. I was always prepared to wait while he did his duty sharing himself with the rest of the world, talked to the reporters. But just like he used to, he makes a beeline for me. The increased fame, pressure to give himself to his fans and the rest of the world, it hasn't changed his priorities one bit. He wants that hug I'm itching for just as bad as I do.

I try and fail at not being dramatic. His grin is huge as he walks toward me, and I can't hide my own. I break into a jog and throw myself at him, wrapping my arms around his neck, my legs around his waist. I'm so damn proud of him.

JACE

Wes told me about Madeline and Stephanie at dinner while the girls were distracted, giggling about some kid who tried hitting on Angel in front of Tanner.

The news threatened to ruin the cloud of happy I'd been riding all day, but I knew Wes was just having my back, making sure I was in the loop so I wasn't caught off guard by anything later.

"Dude, I don't think Pepper was fazed in the least. She's cool as a cucumber around the bitches that never seem to leave her alone."

Wes didn't hide his awe. My brother had a thing for Pepper way back when, and while I always appreciated his protectiveness of her, it used to piss me off too because I thought he still had feelings for her. Now, I saw it was more of a brotherly protectiveness. Hell, maybe it was all along and my own love for our girl distorted everything. Jealousy could make all of us act like assholes.

I'd known for years now that the admiration he had for Pepper wasn't rooted in the kind of emotions I needed to be jealous about. And it wasn't only because he was married to Pepper's best friend now. Nah, I could see Wes truly looked at Pepper like family. There was no lust or want there. Just the desire that she had the best, that she was happy.

"Our girl's come a long fucking way, hasn't she?" I asked. As if sensing we were talking about her, she glanced our way.

"Turned into one fierce woman. Hell, she kind of scares *me* sometimes. She didn't even bother throwing down with those bitches. Just wanted to get her snacks and watch you play." Wes chuckled and shook his head.

Pepper got up from the other end of the table. We were in a private room with the Snyders and the Walkers. After a steak dinner, we topped it off by ordering a slew of desserts, and the women shuffled around seats to try all the dishes.

As she made her way toward us, my mouth went dry seeing her in my jersey. It hung off her petite frame, but somehow managed to be sexier than just about anything else she could be wearing. I knew my wife's body better than my own so it was easy to imagine what was underneath. And now I was hard as a rock. Damn.

When Pepper decided to take a seat in my lap, it didn't help the situation. She squirmed in reaction to discovering my plight and I grasped her hip, trying to keep her from torturing me.

She had told me she was proud of me at least a dozen times tonight, but now it was my turn. I might have been focused on the game, but Denise made sure to email me the Times article about my wife as soon as we hit the locker rooms.

It hadn't surprised me Pepper hadn't even read it yet when I brought it up earlier. Even with a job requiring frequent social media contact, she had always been able to ignore her phone and emails when there was something else important to her going on.

"They called your performance yesterday the 'epitome of what sport is all about.'" She had told me she'd paced her teammates, and I'd known that was a sacrifice given this was meant to be a comeback race of sorts for her, a chance to redeem her reputation. Of course, my girl would end up redeeming herself entirely unintentionally just by doing her thing, following her heart.

"They weren't wrong. They didn't need to focus on me so much. Indy, Kendra and Maisy were helping too, but they got the teamwork part right. Honestly, Jace?" She turned to look at me. "That race meant more to me than hitting the podium at the world cross championships, or any of the big races I've done around the world. It was more fun too."

"And you're still riding the high, aren't you?" I could sense it, that unique energy that vibrates from Pep after a breakthrough workout or a good race. She was practically glowing with it tonight.

"That and from your game, too." She rested her forehead on mine, and when her hand inched below my shirt, my muscles tensed at her touch. Pep ran her hand over my stomach until it rested atop the Baby Wilder tattoo. "It feels like a betrayal to our baby to say this, but I feel like everything's come together for us."

She was already pressed against me, but I pulled her even closer. "It's okay to be happy, Pep," I reminded her, and myself.

"I miss the path I thought we were headed on when I found out we were pregnant. I'm still grieving it. But at the same time, I love the path we've found, where we're headed now." Pepper's voice cracked as she tried to say what she was feeling.

"I know, baby."

Her hand curled around my chest and she blinked a few times. I was already thinking about growing our family again, could hardly wait to make another baby with this woman, but I didn't share my thoughts. Google had told me that one of the worst things someone can say to a woman after a miscarriage was not to worry because you'll have more. I knew it wasn't the same thing, telling her I was excited for more babies. It wasn't as if I was dismissing the loss of our first, but still, I needed to tread carefully.

Pep surprised me by voicing my own thoughts. "I'm going to train my ass off for the trials, but if I don't make the team, it won't be so bad, because then we can start making another baby right away."

I forced myself to remember we were in a room with other people. "That's really not helping the situation pressing into your ass right now, Pep."

My heart was soaring too. We'd talked about having children in the future in a couple of sessions with Nancy, but it felt slightly forced and clinical. Like we had to address the elephant in the room to keep moving forward. It helped, sure, but I still wasn't sure Pep's heart was entirely on board. As I watched color fill her cheeks, I knew that she was starting to feel the same excitement I was for the future of our family.

Chapter Twenty-Seven

PEPPER

The day has finally arrived. The Olympic marathon trials. My first marathon. I expected to be more nervous than I've ever been for a race in my life, but it's the opposite. As I strip off my warm-ups with five minutes until the start, a calmness washes through my bones. I've put in the miles. Hammered out 5:40 mile pace on long training runs and sat in terribly uncomfortable ice baths to help recover afterward. Pushed my body to distances beyond anything I've conquered before. I know that I'll give it everything today, but that when it comes to the marathon, it's hard to say how I'll respond to all that training. For some runners, it takes years of marathon training blocks like the one I just went through before they see the results.

Instead of analyzing my race plan or the state of my muscles and body, I've found myself thinking about Baby Wilder all morning. He or she would have been born by now, just a little nugget. I still miss the baby I never met. My hand presses to my chest, where I've got a tattoo like Jace's. I didn't care that it was cliché to get a matching tattoo with my husband. I loved seeing it on Jace so much, and touched it all the time; I wanted one in the same spot, right where I felt Baby Wilder on a daily basis.

I don't know if Jace knows I do this, but I take over-the-counter pregnancy tests regularly. Usually right before a hard workout, and today, before racing my first marathon. I need the peace of mind that I'm not hurting a baby before I run hard and push my body to its limits.

There's a hand on my shoulder. "Pep?" It's Lexi.

"Yup. Ready." I glance over to find most of the runners in the elite field already at the start line.

"Baby Wilder would be three months now, right?" she asks softly.

I smile. "Yeah." I love that she saw where my hand was clutching and didn't dismiss it. She knows that everything could have been different, and that as much as I love where I am and what I'm doing, I can't help the sadness that seeps in when I think about what it would be like if I hadn't miscarried.

Lexi doesn't try to tell me to stop thinking about it, she just offers a hug and I take it. "Come on, girl, let's go run a marathon."

A minute later, the gun goes off, and I find my spot near the front of the pack. Today is about placing in the top three. It's not about running a certain time, and I need to stay focused on the runners around me more so than usual. The first half of the race is slightly faster than I expected. I've trained to run 5:40 pace – just under a 2:30 marathon, which may or may not be a top-three time depending on the day. There are at least two dozen women here today who could run sub-2:30 marathons on the right day. Some already have.

We hit the half marathon mark at 1:12, which is actually 5:30 pace. There's a strong possibility I'll blow up at some point in the second half, but I can't back down. I have to stay with this lead group and see if I've got what it takes. Indy is the only other one of my teammates still in the pack. Two Olympic team veterans are pushing the pace, and while I'm willing to follow them, most of the other runners have dropped off. There are only six of us going into the second half, which doesn't mean anything yet. In the marathon, the real racing starts around mile twenty-one or twenty-two. It's entirely possible the chase pack will overtake us at that point, so I'm not about to get complacent.

I'm guessing the two veteran Olympic marathoners ahead of us are pushing the pace as an intimidation strategy. Or because they know some of the younger runners have more speed. Doubt it though, the marathon almost never comes down to a sprint finish. The women train together in Oregon, with the group Kendra used to train with. The two of them are working together to push the pace, hoping to drop us, but we hold on.

When we pass a table with our water bottles, I almost miss mine. We've practiced grabbing bottles and drinking during training runs, but it's harder to do it in a pack than I'm prepared for. I end up slowing down to make sure I'm grabbing the bottle with my name on it. It's got the right formula in it that my stomach tolerates, and at this point in the race it's crucial I get some in my system. By the time I get it down and toss it to the side, a gap has formed between me and the lead runners.

With my legs starting to fatigue, it's so tempting to look back and let the chase group catch me, run with them the rest of the race. Aside from the two veterans going strong, the rest of the lead pack has dispersed. Water stops will do that, and often they don't regroup. I'm uncertain what to do here. I could regroup with Indy and the two other women who fell off the lead pack just now, create our own chase group. Or, I could pick it up to go after the two veterans and stick with them. It's mile sixteen now, and I don't know if it's smart to use energy to catch the women. But if I stick with a chase pack, I'm also taking a risk. Without the veterans pushing the pace, we're likely to be caught by the others, and then it really is likely to come down to a sprint finish for the third spot on the team.

When I hear Bunny and Lulu screaming at the top of their lungs, and then spot them jumping up and down and waving pom-poms, my legs make the decision for me. Those ladies don't know a thing about race strategy, but they're yelling at me to hurry up and catch the leaders, and before I know it, that's exactly what I'm doing. They road-tripped it down here, and I want to take this risk for them.

When I finally catch back up, the leaders hear me and glance over their shoulders, not hiding their surprise. It's clear they were hoping to drop the rest of us and secure their positions on the team before the final few miles put us all to the test. Nope. I'm still hanging on.

I've got no way of knowing if that was a stupid move, but here I am. Yeah, my body is already hurting in a way it never has before, and I've still got a lot of miles left, but I've trained distances longer than this, and I'm confident that what I'm feeling isn't a sign I'm going to blow up. At least not yet.

There's a small uphill at mile twenty, and Jace is waiting for me at the top, urging me on. As we work our way up the hill, the pace slows slightly, and I realize that the Olympians pacing me are starting to feel the consequences of twenty miles at a brutal pace.

I'm in pain too, but seeing my husband clap his hands and shout encouragements, it makes me smile. I can't help but notice that some on the sidelines are more interested in him than the lead pack of runners coming through. He did play in the Super Bowl last weekend. If my husband wasn't already hot shit, he sure as hell is now. They didn't win, but he's got plenty of years ahead of him to get all his goals.

I'm expecting the pace to pick up again once the road flattens out, but the veterans don't attack again. They've eased back, and I can only assume it's because they're toast. After all, with 10K left, this is when the race in a marathon really begins. When the training under our belts is really put to the test. I've run 6.2 miles a million times, but the distance ahead is daunting. Especially as the women I've been following start to falter, and I realize it's time for me to set the pace and take the lead if I don't want the others to catch us.

We can't hear the chase pack behind us, but it's hard to say what the gap is. It's not like we have earpieces updating us like they do in cycling races. And anyway, it wouldn't make a difference. We're going to need to dig deep just to get to the finish line, never mind if we're a mile ahead of the others or about to get overtaken. So I let the two veterans fall into line behind me as I attempt to hold the 5:30 pace they've been pushing for twenty miles.

I can't quite pull it off. I know I've slowed the pace, even without looking at my watch. My legs burn, begging me to slow to a jog, or just stop altogether. Every muscle in my body is cramping, and the world around me is blurring. Not in a way that makes me think I'm going to faint again, but in a way that makes me focus all my energy on simply continuing to move forward. Tunnel vision. Thoughts of pacing, and strategy, and the runners behind me, it all goes to the wayside as I use every cell in my body to keep going.

It's not only my legs burning, it's my arms, chest, throat, hell, even my eyes. By the time we hit the final mile, I register enough from the noise bearing down on me that I'm alone now. It's only my name I hear shouted, not the others. Squinting, I try to focus on the road ahead. Did runners pass without me noticing? It's entirely possible. I'm half delirious. But I don't see anything. Just an empty road.

The realization that I am winning the Olympic Trials marathon shoots much-needed adrenaline though my system. The zing of energy shakes some clarity into my head and I let the cheers fuel me forward. As I close in on the finish line, it really dawns on me. I'm going to win the Olympic Trials marathon. I'm going to be an Olympian. Tears stream down my face and I completely forget about the pain I'm in as a smile spreads. My hands go to my mouth in disbelief when I break the tape. When I stumble to the ground, it's not from exhaustion – well, that too, but it's the shock of what I just did that brings me to my knees. My hands go to my chest, clinging to Baby Wilder.

Familiar arms are around me, lifting me up, and I breathe in my husband. He rented a scooter just so he could cheer at the top of the hill, the hardest part of the course, and still race through the side streets to get to the finish before me. And my strong man has tears in his eyes too.

His words melt over me. "I guess I'll have to wait another six months before I get to put a baby in you."

EPILOGUE

16 YEARS LATER

"Dad, how can you be cool with a purple house? It's fucking embarrassing," I hear Jude ask as I walk through the sliding back door to our deck. Jace looks up from the grill and smiles at me before answering our fifteen-year-old son.

"Don't curse in front of your mom. And she earned a fucking purple house when she won an Olympic medal. Before you were even born."

Jude is a mini Jace. The oldest of our four kids, he's starting his sophomore year at Brockton Public tomorrow. And he's been embarrassed of our purple house since kindergarten.

"I can't believe you made that promise. You should have known better. Of course she was going to win a fucking medal."

"Don't curse in front of your sister," Jace scolds as Dash, our second oldest, approaches from the yard with Josie on his hip after pushing her on the tree swing. Jace really hasn't cleaned up his language since becoming a father, but feels the need to reprimand the kids when they talk just like him. With neither of us growing up in "normal families" consisting of two parents or siblings, we're winging this thing. And, after a sixteen-year career in the NFL, it's no wonder Jace hasn't cleaned up his mouth.

Our only daughter and youngest of the four is also a mini Jace, only a girl version. She refuses to wear anything but the kid-size Wilder jerseys the Stallions had made for all our kids over the years. Josie is only three years old, and adores her older brothers. Gran tries to get her to take on her eclectic style involving animal prints and neon but Josie isn't into it.

With four kids each four years apart, Gran's busier cooking and taking care of us than ever before. Now in her nineties, she's still living on Shadow Lane with Lulu. Wallace and Harold passed away within months of each other three years ago, but Gran and Lulu show no signs of slowing down. Without their help, and Jim's too, I don't know if Jace and I could have continued chasing our athletic goals and had four kids. Well, we could have, but it wouldn't have given the kids the stability we wanted for them. We tried to avoid being out of town at the same time as much as possible, but it happened a couple of times a year. Gran, Lulu, Jim, or Wes and Zoe took the kids when that happened, and the kids loved it so much they probably wished it happened more often.

After the first Olympics, Jace had not been kidding about putting a baby in me. He took his promise seriously, setting an alarm to ensure time for sex before heading to the stadium for practice, and then rushing home to me afterward to continue the baby-making activities. When his efforts were fruitful, he made it his mission to repeat the task after each Olympics, except this last one. At forty years old, I don't feel the need to endure another high-risk pregnancy when I already have four children. Besides, I always liked even numbers better. Jude and Zane share May birthdays, exactly eight years apart. Dash turned eleven in June, and Josie turned three in July.

While Jude and Josie have trouble written all over them, Dash wants to be a runner like me. Zane, well... He has a lot of Bernadette Jones in him and walks to the beat of a different drum altogether. He joins us just as we're sitting down for dinner, wearing polka-dotted suspenders over a tie-dyed shirt and faded jeans that look suspiciously like a pair I used to wear in elementary school.

"Did Granny B give those jeans to you?" I ask as I scoop pasta salad onto his plate. Gran refuses to be called a great-grandma, so she goes by Granny B with her great-grandkids.

"Yeah. She gave me a box of clothes. Said they're vintage. I got these shoes too. Like 'em?" He pulls up his jeans to display a pair of blue high top Chucks.

"Zane, those were your mom's shoes when she was your age," Jace tells him with amusement.

Zane grins. "Cool. I'm testing out my outfit for the first day tomorrow. I'll tell everyone that my Olympian mom used to wear these."

The kid's incredibly sweet, and I'm grateful he's got the Wilder build and has two older brothers. I worry that his eccentricities will get him bullied at school. Jace tells me that's ridiculous, and he's probably right. So far, Zane has proven to be the most popular kid in his class every year. He makes friends with everyone. But he's still in elementary school and I know firsthand how mean kids can be.

For a kid who's been embarrassed of our purple house for ten years, Jude isn't the least bit embarrassed of his eccentric little brother. In fact, Jude loves bringing his younger siblings around with him, having them watch his football and baseball practices and games.

"I want to go to school!" Josie complains from her spot between Jace and Jude.

"You get to hang with Dad all day," Dash reminds her.

Passing the corn on the cob down the table, I tell her, "You'll start preschool soon, baby, as soon as Daddy decides he'll give you up for a few hours each day."

After retiring three years ago, Jace has taken on the role of stay-at-home dad, and while the rest of the kids started preschool at Josie's age, Jace refuses to sign her up to start this year. I haven't pushed it. She's our last, and the two of them have a special bond.

I've just returned from my fifth, and final, Olympic games.

"Hey Mom," Dash asks, "can we go on a run tomorrow before school?"

Our dog, Pretzel, perks up at the word "run" and nudges my knee from under the table. Dave ran up until the day before he passed away at age twelve. Even though Jude was a toddler and climbing all over everything, it still felt like the house was missing something so we got a puppy, which Jude named Dave Junior. DJ passed away two years ago, and now we've got Pretzel.

"Course, Dash, wouldn't miss it." We started doing sunrise runs together on the first day of school a few years ago. He's starting middle school, and I wonder when he'll decide he's too cool to run with me, but Jace thinks that will never happen. Dash still idolizes me and wants to be an Olympian someday, but I don't know how long that will last. I keep expecting the kids to become embarrassed of us some day, but even Jude still wants to hang out with us.

I would run every day with Dash but I'm doing my best to keep him from overdoing it too young. I can tell he's inherited my love for running, but I also don't want him to feel any pressure just because of who his parents are.

"Cruz said you're retiring now. Is that true?" Dash asks, concern furrowing his brow.

Jace laughs. "Your cousin likes to rile you up. Uncle Wes used to do the same to me. Especially when it came to your mom."

"Mom's never going to retire, dummy," Jude tells his brother.

Jace shoots Jude a warning look and Jude mumbles an apology before saying under his breath, "It was a dumb fucking question."

I sigh. "I'll be running as long as my legs let me," I admit. "And I'll probably always race here and there, but my goals are changing. I'll be doing more coaching with the team instead of racing."

After five Olympics and four kids, I'm ready to slow down. Just a little. I've kept my traveling and racing schedule significantly less demanding than most professional runners in order to be home with the kids and give them as much stability as possible. It's probably one of the reasons I've been able to run relatively injury-free for so long.

"Granny B!" Josie squeals, hopping down from her seat and running across the yard. Pretzel hustles behind her. Gran walks along the sidewalk and opens the side gate to our yard. It's a short walk from Shadow Lane, and I think the kids keep her younger than most in their nineties. She has a reason to crouch down on her knees, like she does now, to give Josie and Pretzel a hug.

Jim, Gran and Lulu have open invitations to dinner at our house, and at least one of them pops in nearly every night. Gran takes her usual spot on our outdoor dinner table between Dash and Zane. It's a little crammed, but that's how we like it best.

"So Jude, you tell your parents about your new girlfriend yet?" Gran asks, reaching to grab a burger and a bun.

My eyes swing to Jude, who attempts to look unfazed, and then to Jace, who is clenching his jaw. "We talked about this, Jude. No girls. They're trouble."

"Real trouble," Gran chimes in. "Might make you paint your house purple someday."

Jace sighs and put down his fork. "Exactly. He can't understand that concept yet. When he understands why I let Pep paint the house purple, he can have a girlfriend."

"She's not my girlfriend," Jude says with conviction.

"I saw you kissing her," Dash adds helpfully. "It was definitely a girl-friend kind of kiss."

Jude shrugs, not even the least bit embarrassed of himself. "I'll just tell her I can't have a girlfriend yet," he replies with a smug expression.

Oh, I don't think so. I see where he's going with this. We have a little player on our hands.

"You need to think of all girls like you think about your sister." Jace tries a new tactic. "Until you're eighteen, at least."

Zane asks through a huge bite, "But Daddy, Josie can't date until she's sixty, I thought?"

Jace takes a long pull of beer. His eyes meet mine over the bottle and I try and fail not to smile. I convey with my eyes that we'll talk about this later. Jace has turned out to be the stricter parent. Some-times, I find it ridiculous given his own activities growing up, but I get it. He made a lot of mistakes he doesn't want to see his kids make. And that control thing, it hasn't changed much even as he's tried to accept that when it comes to kids, there's a lot we can't, and shouldn't try, to control. It's a constant challenge, but one we work on together. The best challenge we have in our lives.

Later, after the kids clear the table, and Gran and the older ones are helping the younger ones get ready for bed, Jace cages me behind the sink. His softs lips brush along my neck. "Hey, Pep." His voice vibrates along my skin and my body instantly reacts. I shut off the water and turn around in his arms.

"Hi." We sneak moments when we can, and Jace is always looking for openings to touch me without kids around. His lips brush mine. "I miss you," I tell him. We live together, see each other every day, sleep together every night, but with four kids, I rarely have my husband's full attention all to myself. Who am I kidding? I can never get enough of this man. Even before kids it was the same way.

"Mmm-hmm," Jace agrees as his hands slide under my shirt.

My hands run down his back, landing on one of my favorite spots. His butt. I grasp the firm muscles, and he thrusts forward, letting me know he's hard as a rock. I lean back, and his kisses trail down my neck, while one of his hands lifts my leg up.

"Daddy? Mommy?" Zane's voice asks from the other side of the kitchen. I'm thankful the kitchen island is at least blocking part of his view. Jace slowly lowers my leg and takes a step back. My body aches for that firmness again, and I try to shake the lust from my head. Zane continues, "Josie can't find her race car pajama bottoms. Do you know where they are?"

"They're in the wash, sweetie," I tell him.

"I'll help her find another pair," Jace offers after discreetly adjusting himself. We all know how ugly it can get when it comes to Josie's pajama choices. Jace is usually the one who can calm her down when a meltdown starts.

He puts a hand on Zane's shoulder as they walk up the stairs side by side. "I don't get why she won't wear her princess nightgown. The ribbons on the arms are cool."

"I don't know, bud. We all like what we like."

Jace glances over his shoulder and finds me leaning on the bannister, smiling dreamily at his ass.

"Love you, Pep," he calls down.

"Love you too, Jace Wilder."

ALSO BY ALI DEAN

Made in the USA
Middletown, DE
16 July 2019